LetsChat

A Novel of Techno-Science, Romance, and Abuse

BELLA E. TAN

CONTENTS

1	Zhu Li-An or Julianne	1
2	Project X Inverted	14
3	LetsChat	21
4	The Date	34
5	Harbin Interlude	48
6	Xter Trials	51
7	An (Un)Natural Selection	73
8	Mao's Miracle	80
9	Glimpses of a Past	92
10	Video Chat	94
11	The Confrontation	107
12	The World of Realms	113
13	Love in an Online Bubble	121
14	A Beijing Promise	136
15	The Bite of Reality	153
16	The Final Exit	170

PROLOGUE

White disappeared. Just like that.

A few nights before, his message "You've come to the mainland?" had come sliding down the top of her Samsung Galaxy S6. Li-An had changed to a different sim card in case he tried to call her on the one she'd used for the last SMS. Still, White managed to return her message via a different route: LetsChat. Li-An clicked on the three horizontally-aligned dots that formed the right icon on White's profile page, but couldn't make up her mind whether to press "block". She was still fiddling with the command options when, in front of her eyes, his profile just vanished.

Franticly, Li-An messaged Grey and coaxed him into helping her experiment with the LetsChat settings, without telling him why. First, she'd delete him. Then he'd make a friend request, followed by a message. Any message. A minute later, he'd delete her. No, that wasn't the correct formula. Ok, start over. They'd add each other back, only that this time Li-An would delete him. But Grey's profile didn't vanish as White's just had. Something else was wrong.

Had he sensed what she was feeling, and removed her before she did him? But hadn't the experiment with Grey ruled out that scenario? Was it a technical glitch? Or worse, had he reported her, and had her permanently blacklisted?

What did it really matter? She needed it to end. What did it matter who's fault it was?

1 ZHU LI-AN OR JULIANNE

"Where is your man?" Startled, Li-An quickly made a search for that damn gadget. There on the screen was Evans, looking all stern and serious.

"I've got him. It's just a matter of time," Li-An replied. Her voice quivered with fear.

"But you don't have much time, Li-An." Evans gave her an even sterner look.

"I know but . . ." Before she could finish her sentence, Evans switched himself off.

"I know! I know! I know! Stop reminding me!" Frustrated, Li-An switched off her RexPad. She shifted her gaze to the mirror standing by the balcony, and for a long time stared at her own image.

Li-An had always been pretty, but didn't know it when she was growing up, or for a long time after that. She had soft feminine features, a well-proportioned figure, and large breasts for a Chinese. Her most alluring feature was a well-defined curve in her lower back, accentuating her rear end as she walked. But now at 39, Li-An was very aware of her beauty, and that she looked much younger than her age. Her muscle tone was excellent and her skin firm and taut. Even though she worked late into the night on her PhD dissertation, she'd kept her thick, luscious hair, while most of her male colleagues were starting to bald. At the last alumni dinner at Kramen University, she'd stood out in a snug, daring red lace cheongsam. With hardly any wrinkles, Li-An could easily pass as a twenty-something college student. When asked how she did it, her answers sounded like they'd come straight from a textbook. A combination of exercise (yoga in her case), monthly facials, good organic diet, a strict detox regime, a full eight-hour sleep every night, et cetera. Or simply good genes.

These answers always deflected conversation back to safer topics. No one would have believed the reality. And she was forbidden to tell them in any case.

How unlikely to end up like this, she often thought. Li-An had been stripped of so much confidence in her youth. It started with her surname, Zhu which sounded exactly like "pig" in Chinese, and caused so much teasing through her pre-tertiary years. She couldn't change that, but in college, Li-An picked out an English name – Julianne - that sounded close to her Chinese one. It gave her a sense of starting fresh with a new identity. Indeed, her grades began spiralling up. She made the Dean's List three years in a row, and in her final year was awarded a scholarship to Tokyo University, where she'd go on to master the Japanese language.

But Li-An wasn't street smart, unfortunately. And so, when a strikingly good-looking classmate took an interest in her, she was taken in. He'd fetch her to school every morning in his swanky Mazda MX-5 and send her love letters. His address, on the high-end eastern side of Kramen Island, was embossed on the back of all his envelopes. Li-An's parents were certainly impressed. "This guy comes from a good family." They'd even told her to give up her studies and marry him if he proposed. "It's no use for a girl to study too much. You'll eventually have to get married." But to Li-An's surprise, the man told her he'd wait till she finished her scholarship year in Japan.

"I want you to be prepared for Tokyo," her boyfriend told her one day, suggesting that he and his family bring her to see Japan before she began her scholarship year. "Since you've never taken a plane, it'll be a good orientation. You'll know what a 'gate' means and learn how to ask for a window seat at the check-in counter." Li-An really was quite naive. It didn't occur to her then that her boyfriend was more complicated than he appeared. She asked if they were sleeping in separate rooms. "Same room but two single beds," was his reply. She was still hesitant – she hadn't known him very long. But her boyfriend appeared at her doorstep one evening when her family was having dinner, dressed in neatly pressed suit and necktie. He'd even sprayed on cologne. The guy was not only polite but could hold an intelligent conversation on Kramen politics (he was a political science major) and soon Li-An heard her father agreeing to his holiday proposition. When she shared her concerns with her mother later that night, she was told it was her responsibility to protect herself in the hotel room. "Wear a pad even if you're not on your period," was her mom's advice for when they were alone. "Since he's so good-looking, no harm enjoying yourself. But no sex. You need to stay a virgin until the night of your wedding." Li-An had heard her mom give the same advice to her older sister, so didn't think it unusual. On the day that they were scheduled to fly, her mother called her aunts – all four of them – to announce her departure. But it was really to brag that her daughter now had a rich boyfriend and would soon get hitched.

It began as soon as they were in flight, when he reached out to touch Li-An's breasts. She was covered in the airline blanket so the act was discreet. Li-An looked to her right and saw that his eyes were closed, though his right hand was actively caressing her. She turned to look at her own reflection in the window. There were smudges of tears on her blanket. He withdrew the hand after a few long moments and she soon fell asleep.

The plane touched down at Tokyo Narita International Airport the next morning. After clearing immigration, Li-An, her boyfriend, his family and the group that'd signed up for the tour package gathered around the guide, who was waving a flag carrying the company's name. They were herded onto a bus which would bring them to their first destination, the Asakusa Shrine. The tour company must have thought it a waste of valuable time to bring tourists straight to the hotel to rest, so had packed their first day in Japan with activities. The guide's advice was to use the bus ride to catch up on their sleep between stops. But Li-An was too excited by the scene outside the bus window. After all, it was her first overseas trip. She found the soothing pastels of Tokyo – from the light blue sky to the off-white walls lining the expressway as they headed into the city – a striking contrast to the vivid emerald jade of her country, tropical Kramen Island. Her boyfriend was holding Li-An tightly in his arms. He'd even made her rest her head on his left shoulder. Whenever she'd raise her head to look out of the window, he'd instantly tilt it back to its original place. From that position, Li-An spotted his father eyeing her surreptitiously from the seat next to them.

"Once we reach the hotel, I want to buy a phone card," Li-An told her boyfriend. It was the late 1990s and the smart phone had yet to be invented. "Why?" He asked. "I want to call a friend," she said, "he's a Kramean doing his PhD at Tokyo University. We were introduced by his cousin last semester when he returned home. I'm thinking since I'm here we should meet and catch up," Li-An chattered away, innocently, until she saw the change in his face. "And what about me?" he asked. Li-An didn't know what to say, except that the man was just an acquaintance, nothing more. Her boyfriend retracted his arms, and Li-An was left sitting by herself close to the window. When she turned to look at him a few minutes later, he was twitching his eyes as if to stop tears from flowing. His legs fidgeted so distractingly that his mother began to take notice. Even his younger brother, who was sitting behind the parents, saw the change in his behaviour but quickly turned his gaze away. He wanted to avoid Li-An's eyes, which were fishing around for some kind of an answer.

Soon, the tour guide rose from her seat and announced they'd reached the shrine. Everyone was getting ready to alight when the bus stopped, but her boyfriend didn't flinch. "Are you alright?" Li-An was getting scared. He shook his head, but didn't look at her. "We're at the shrine. Shouldn't we be getting out of the bus?" she asked. He slowly rose from his seat and made for the exit, and Li-An quietly followed behind. For the rest of the day, he didn't utter a single word. Neither did he hold Li-An's hand as they made their way through the historical sites packing the day's itinerary. Instead he trailed behind the whole group, his head drooped low. His hands were tucked into the side pockets of his pants, as if to signal he was deep in troubled thought. The man's parents were obviously worried. They occasionally turned to talk to him but were given the cold shoulder. "Is he always like that?" Li-An asked the younger brother, who only shrugged and walked away.

Dinner was followed by a brief walk to their hotel in Ikebukuro, a bustling district full of pachinko parlors. The suitcases had been unloaded from the bus and lined up with disturbing neatness in the hotel lobby. The tour guide headed straight for the front desk and within ten minutes gathered everyone to distribute the room cards.

She called out the name of the younger brother and handed him three cards. Obviously, she'd already identified family groups. The brother then handed one card to his parents, one to Li-An's boyfriend, and kept the last one for himself. There was no duplicate for her. Her boyfriend took Li-An's hand – the first time since that morning – and headed for the elevator. The suitcases would be sent to their room later.

Thankfully there were two single beds, as he'd said there'd be. Nevertheless, Li-An felt uneasy. It was the first time she was alone with a man in a hotel room. She chose the bed closer to the bathroom and sat at one corner, her eyes wandering over the furnishings. The awkward silence was broken by a knock on the door. A young male Japanese porter entered with two suitcases and lightly placed them on the floor next to Li-An's feet. He then uttered a string of Japanese syllables she understood, but which eluded her boyfriend, who had little knowledge of the language. "Arigato gozaimasu," he nevertheless replied for both of them. Alone now with Li-An, he reached for his suitcase, unlocked the safety code, and pulled out a set of pyjamas and fresh underwear. "I'll go shower."

When it was Li-An's turn to shower, she made sure to lock the bathroom door before undressing and stepping into the bathtub. As soon as water gushed out from the shower head, she burst into tears, but continued to wash herself. She stepped out of the bathtub, making sure not to slip and fall, and grabbed the neatly folded hotel towel to dry herself. Before putting on her pyjamas, she made sure to wear her bra. But she didn't follow her mother's advice to wear a sanitary pad, thinking she could protect herself without it. Li-An then dabbed dry her hair with the towel and applied moisturizer on her face. When she opened the door, Li-An was startled. Her boyfriend was standing directly in front of it with a weird expression on his face: mouth wide open, and raised eyelids revealing the upper sclera. One of his legs was slightly raised and the foot flexed, as though he'd been leaning against the door, and would have fallen had she opened it a moment earlier. It was the second time in a matter of hours he'd behaved in ways she'd never seen, and couldn't understand.

He turned Li-An around and lightly pushed her back into the bathroom. "Your hair isn't entirely dry. You can't even take care of yourself." He then pulled out the hotel's hair dryer and started to blow-dry her. Li-An had cut her long hair short just before the trip so it didn't take long. When he was finished, he led Li-An to her bed, laid her down, and covered her with the quilt from the shoulders down. She felt like a doll he was playing with. He then tucked her in tightly, making sure she was as thoroughly wrapped as an Egyptian mummy.

Li-An didn't like the feeling of being man-handled, so chose that moment to start discussing what had happened that morning. "I didn't quite like how you behaved today," she said. "I told you there was nothing to be jealous about. If you continue to be like that, chances are we'll eventually break up."

Still looking down at her from the side of the bed, her boyfriend immediately fell into a hysterical display of emotion. First came a series of suppressed whimpers, followed by convulsive gasps of excessive sobbing. "Are you alright?" Li-An felt scared, guilty, and helpless. Suddenly he jumped onto her, pinning her down with the weight of his body, and pulling down the quilt that he'd so neatly arranged moments before. He started forcefully rubbing Li-An's breasts through her clothes, moving back and forth between them. She tried to push his hands away, but he raised her arms and pressed them together over her head. He held them there with one hand, while unbuttoning her shirt and removing her bra with the other. At the same time, he spread open her legs using his right foot. Looking down her body, he saw Li-An half naked for the first time. "You have a nice slim figure," he said. With his free hand, he unbuttoned his shirt and pressed his exposed upper torso against hers, making sounds of ecstatic relief. He kept talking as he groped and suckled Li-An's breasts for what seemed to her like an hour. "You're twenty-one now. You should enjoy yourself," he said, and "You know, I already see you as my wife."

When Li An woke early the next morning, he was sleeping next to her on her single bed. She saw that her breasts were exposed and remembered what had happened the night before. She was wondering why she'd not put up more of a fight when his eyes started to slowly twitch open. "Hey, I love you," he said. He got out of bed, then searched under the quilt for his pyjama top. She noted that he still had his pants on. Li-An glanced down to see if she was wearing hers. She was, which confirmed they didn't have sex. As she slowly raised herself up, her pyjama top with only the two lower buttons still intact fell halfway to her elbow. Li-An noticed two bite marks on each of her breasts close to the nipples. "I want you to remember me. And don't see that man," she recalled him saying the night before as he bit hard into her skin. Now he came and sat next to her, helped her on with her shirt, kissed her on the forehead, and told her to go wash her face.

For the next six nights, her boyfriend forcibly made out with Li-An in each of their Japanese hotel rooms, a different one each day as they travelled to new destinations. "I don't think this is right," Li-An told him each time he approached her bed. "But you are my wife," he'd always reply. On the seventh night, she resisted him. "Ouch! That hurts! What are you doing!" Li-An pushed his hand away from her vagina even though she had her underwear on. "I'm trying to give you pleasure. So you can have a good night's sleep," he said. "I don't want. And I don't know what that is. Just go away!" He did, and for the first time slept in his own bed.

On the flight back to Kramen Island, he said to Li-An: "I know you'll leave me once the plane touches down." Li-An pretended not to hear. But he was right. She'd made up her mind not to see him again once she picked up her suitcase at the baggage claim. She'd tell her parents about his jealous temper – and maybe tell her mom about his behaviour in the hotel room – and they'd agree with her decision to break it off with him.

But they didn't. "You should go and spend more time with him," said Li-An's father the next day. He even insisted on driving her to her boyfriend's house. "Is this right?" Li-An asked her father as they drove, alluding to the intimacy she'd be offering the man once inside his house. Of course, she wasn't explicit with her father about what happened in the hotels, out of embarrassment. "Yes" was his short reply. For the next two months, Li-An was subjected to every kind of sexual pressure her boyfriend could think of exerting. One day he told her she was a stick in the mud and pulled her into the bathroom, took her clothes off and began showering her. "You dirty little thing," he said as he rubbed her all over with soap. He held Li-An from behind, and used his right forearm to repeatedly push her breasts up and down, the soap acting as lubricant. "Isn't it fun?" Li-An didn't reply although she certainly felt the sensation. He played with her clitoris one night to the point where she felt guilty for enjoying it, and ended up sliding down to the bottom of the bed, feeling scared. She'd now begun spending nights at her boyfriend's house at his insistence. There was no objection from his parents. As for Li-An's mom, she just kept telling her "no sex".

Li-An decided to find a summer job, and landed a temporary clerical position at a law firm. "You know, we'll not be able to spend as much time together if you take a job," he told her, his arms rested on the glass barrier overlooking the flight of escalators in Takashimaya, a high-end Japanese department store in Kramen's main shopping district. She feigned regret, but was secretly relieved. Once she had a job, she no longer had to service him during the day, jerking him off as he semi-napped, and wearing the colour black from top to toe at his insistence. He kept telling Li-An to cover herself up because men were such sexual creatures, and black was safest at deflecting attention. He called girls who modestly pressed a hand against their chests when they bent down to pick something up, thus hiding their cleavage, good models for Li-An to emulate. With the day-time job, there was no more letting him put his hands on her private parts as they drove around in his car. Li-An would feel embarrassed if a bus happened to stop next to them and a passenger looked on. But the most bizarre thing he liked to do was squat down and watch her pee while she was sitting on the toilet bowl. He'd look intently through the gap between her knees, spreading them even more to get a good view. "What're you doing?" Li-An reacted embarrassingly the first time he did that. "You're my wife" was his reply.

He even lectured to Li-An after each make-out session on his so-called "ways of the world". The point was often to teach her how screwed up men actually were, as though she needed additional lessons. As for women, he said they were no longer fun sexually once they'd given birth since their "hole" had expanded, and that one's looks were the most important factor in getting ahead in life.

Once she began her job, Li-An's remaining nights with her boyfriend became even stranger, as if he was punishing her for choosing work over him. She woke up one morning with severe bite marks on her breasts. She'd slept soundly the night before but vaguely remembered pain being inflicted on her nipples, as if in a dream. Her boyfriend had not sucked but sank his teeth into Li-An's areola. The bite marks were visible from the thin layer of blood that had congealed overnight. And when she showered, she was seized by sharp pangs of pain as the water hit her chest.

Still, Li-An did not leave him.

By the second month of the relationship, Li-An looked and behaved like a different person. She began to adopt some of his thoughts and even dressed – or rather, covered – herself the way he wanted without complaint. She also stopped doing the things he disliked. When he was pursuing her, Li-An had lightly touched the front mirror of his car. A few days later, he politely asked her in one of his love letters to stop. He wrote in the voice of his car, which he called Max. "It tickles," was the reason he gave her, and Li-An was charmed. Now, however, he'd react angrily if Li-An's hair or arms accidentally brushed against any of Max's window glass. One afternoon she'd rested her arm on the window sill of the door and her elbow touched the glass without her sensing it. He quickly pulled to the side of the expressway, then jerked Li-An towards him with a force that took her by surprise. Simultaneously he reached across her and incessantly wiped the glass where it had come in contact with her elbow. "So, the thing about Max being itchy. It's not just a joke?" she asked. "Why's it taken you so long to figure that out!" he shouted.

The biting continued. One day, Li-An decided to confide in her sister, who was a year older. She took off her shirt to reveal her bite marks. Even the earliest ones were still visible in the form of bruises. "What a bastard!" Her sister then called him up. They would meet the next day. Li-An knew her boyfriend would dress well for the occasion and hoped that her sister would not be taken in by his outward charm. She waited all day for her sister to return, and when she finally did late that night, Li-An came running down the stairs. "How did it go?" she asked. "I want to talk to mommy. Go back to your room and sleep," she ordered. Li-An was disturbed by the answer. "But why?" she responded. "Just go back up." Her sister turned into the living room where their mother had dozed off on the sofa. Li-An's family never quite took her seriously – for a reason no one was allowed to talk about – and Li-An was used to it. So when her sister gave a command, Li-An obeyed even if it didn't make sense.

When Li-An woke up the next morning, she found her sister standing in front of the bathroom mirror, busy applying make-up. A saleswoman, Li-An's sister knew the importance of enhancing her physical assets especially her C cup breasts, which she bolstered by wearing dresses with low necklines. She wasn't tall. A mere 1.58 meters. But her collection of swanky stilettos and her long, voluminous hair more than made up for her flaws, and on her second year clinched the company's "Saleswoman of the Year" award. Two Louis Vuitton bags from the latest collection, a white Mercedes-Benz C-Class, and a closet of clothes carrying the tags of luxury brands. In the eyes of their parents, Li-An's sister was the emblem of success.

"Maybe he's right. You're not couple-oriented," was her sister's only comment on her meeting with Li-An's boyfriend the night before. She said it while rolling her eyes and raising her lip to one side with a dismissive expression, all of which Li-An saw in the mirror.

For days, her boyfriend didn't contact Li-An. She finally called him a week later and asked for a meeting. "Meet me at the park near my house," he said. He didn't offer to pick her up so Li--An took public transport instead. His tone on meeting her was cordial but cold, as if she was a stranger. They sat across each other on the only wooden picnic bench in the park. Li-An began to confront him about his bizarre behaviour with her, but he only laughed it off. "My brother and I talked about you, and he agrees with me that it's all your fault!" He pointed his index finger at Li-An and gave her a look of disgust. "By the way, if I were your parents, I'd never have let my daughter go on a holiday with a stranger." With that he got up and walked away. Li-An was left sitting by herself in the park, shaken and confused, her heart faltering.

Back home, her family added salt to the wound. Her parents had chosen to believe his version of their relationship as he'd related it to Li-An's sister. He'd said "she clams up in conversations," which was only because she'd grown suspicious of him and his family. Li-An's sister also said one day with relish: "He thinks that, unlike me, you don't dress well." But Li-An's sister never told her parents about his perverse actions, while her mom's only lingering concern about the episode was whether Li-An had lost her virginity. "Did you give it to him? Answer me!" Her mom had interrogated her one afternoon in the presence of her father and sister. "No," muttered Li-An. He'd said on their very first night in Japan he'd not take Li-

An's virginity. "I only want to make out with you." But he'd also told her his fantasy was that she'd make love to him of her own accord, while he was semi-sleeping. It was clear to her that he was gradually moving towards that goal. He did not love her, she was now certain, but wanted her as an experimental object and would dump her once she left for Japan. He was certainly into French kissing, and was not shy about touching her breasts and vagina through her clothes whenever it suited him. But his face turned a crimson red when he first removed Li-An's panties one afternoon in his room. He looked intently at her as though he was conducting a clinical inspection, and then smelled her scent. "You're wet. You like me," he said. Of course, Li-An was just experiencing a normal biological response. "It's what you're doing to me," she replied matter-of-factly, acutely aware that her bodily reactions were separate from her emotions. But she felt like she'd lost her case when he retorted by saying "You want this too."

Soon after the relationship ended, Li-An left for her year of exchange study in Japan. While she managed to churn out good grades, she cried every night in her hostel room in Tokyo. It was as though her boyfriend had transferred his darkness to her. Often, but especially at night, her stomach clenched, and the feeling of tightness kept her awake. So much so that Li-An found release only by crossing one leg over the other and pressing them so hard that eventually she came. Li-An also felt a strong urge to bite onto something, which she knew came from the memory of having been bitten, and learnt to transfer it out by gripping firmly on the metal bed frame. The nightly ordeal took such a toll on her health that Li-An felt herself aging at a fast rate, and when she returned to Kramen a year later, she was in terrible shape. Highly emaciated, her cheeks had sunken in, and her collar bones had become so prominent that they could easily hold a string of coins. "You look pathetic!" remarked her sister, who was looking even more confident and radiant. And her parents now started calling Li-An 'crazy' because she began fighting and talking back at them, which she'd never done before. By this time Li-An had lost all faith in her family.

One morning, Li-An saw an ad on the Kramen Times. She made a quick phone call to the number that was advertised. After a short inquiry lasting about five minutes, Li-An put the phone down. She immediately packed a few clothes, some toiletries, and stomped out of her house.

Li-An's family never saw her again.

This is what the ad said:

Looking for Volunteers

The Ministry of Health requires 50 volunteers (25 male, 25 female) for a clinical trial.
Must be Kramean citizen. Duration: Two Years

Benefits:
Testing a restorative drug, that will likely produce a more youthful appearance
Will likely decrease exhaustion
Free lodging in attractive testing facility for periods of the trial.
Stipend available

Interested parties please call 28749501

2 PROJECT X INVERTED

Year: 2001. Li-An's age: 24.

At around noon Li-An arrived at the testing facility, which turned out to be a five-star hotel on Kramen's resort island of Sentacruz. She instantly felt an idyllic peace. Gazing past the concierge station, she could look straight through the sprawling hotel lounge to the grounds beyond. On the right was an open-air lily pond, like in a Monet painting. A big swimming pool was on the left, around which a handful of middle-aged foreign tourists were sun-bathing. Li-An was told to sit in the lounge while a staff member went to call the research team. A waiter came and placed a cup of tea in front of her. While waiting for the teabag to steep, she watched a couple roaming peacocks, and listened to the sound of birds chirping. It was particularly hot that day, but the shadows cast by frangipani trees on the lawn outside not only provided shade but added a striking contrast to the tropical greens. Li-An was soon lost in the combination of bright colours and glinting sunlight reflected from the pool.

"Are you Miss Zhu Li-An?" The voice startled Li-An, who looked up to see an extraordinarily beautiful woman with striking Asian features.

"Yes, I am." But Li-An's voice sounded uncertain. Her lack of confidence was in stark contrast to the demeanour of the woman standing in front of her.

"I'll bring you to your room. Follow me, please. I'm Samantha. Samantha Tan."

Li-An checked the woman out as she followed along behind. Tall, approximately 1.68m in height. A curvaceous figure. Her hair was straight, shining, immaculate. Li-An was especially drawn to her pear-shaped buttocks.

"Samantha . . . How do you . . .? I mean, what's your beauty secret?" Li-An risked a forward question as they walked.

The woman half-turned to look at her. Samantha's hair was parted on the right side and her fringe rested diagonally across the forehead. While not fair, her skin had a nice sun-kissed tone. A sign that she must have been hanging out by the pool. When she smiled, her eyes formed slits. Li-An was attracted to the self-assured confidence she exuded as she walked.

Samantha didn't sound either surprised or flattered by Li-An's question, but answered with a detached professional tone. "Oh, you'll find out pretty soon."

They took the lift to the ground floor, then turned right and walked to the farthest end of the corridor. Samantha brushed a key card against the sensor, releasing a beep. She pushed the door handle down and ushered Li-An into the room.

"This'll be yours for the next two years. You're lucky to get a room with a terrace. Someone checked out this morning. Not from our team. An old American couple on vacation. You'll be living amongst tourists, so we expect you to be absolutely discreet about what we're doing. That's rule number one." Samantha gave Li-An a rather too-stern look.

Li-An nodded and turned to look around. It was just a typical hotel room, but did offer the refuge she'd been seeking. Queen size bed with a wooden bed frame, a wardrobe with only a few hangers, and an iron and ironing board. There was, however, one feature that drew Li-An's attention more than the rest. The bathroom tiles. Big, square turquoise ones. There was something peaceful about the tiles, Li-An thought to herself, and decided she'd spend most of her time in the bathroom. Either taking long baths or just sitting in one corner admiring the colour.

"May I know if there's a library?" asked Li-An.

"Well, there's a shelf in the lounge filled with books. Travel books, mainly. And maybe some novels left behind by tourists.

Why do you ask?" Samantha peered at Li-An with curiosity, as though reading books was a peculiar pastime.

"Well, just in case I get bored sometimes. I left my house in a hurry and didn't pack enough to read," replied Li-An.

Samantha looked back down at the clipboard she'd been holding. She went through a list of what looked to be instructions for newcomers.

"Tomorrow you'll go through a round of assessment tests. Don't worry. It's just routine. The day after tomorrow, if everything's ok, you'll start taking the medication. You'll be briefed later but I can tell you that the pills cause certain reactions which differ from subject to subject. We have nurses check on you periodically, twice or three times a day, depending on your condition. If all goes well, soon you'll start to feel like a brand-new person. So, be patient with yourself." Samantha winked at Li-An with an air of either confidence or condescension. Li-An couldn't quite make out which.

"Oh, one more thing. You'll be given a stipend in return for your service. K1,500 per month. And you get Sundays off. Plus, free food and accommodation. Not a bad deal, huh?"

"Yes, I think so," Li-An nodded, albeit hesitantly. "But what exactly do I do?"

"Just relax and be our human subject," replied Samantha, her voice raised slightly and shoulder shrugged for a split second, as though the answer was obvious.

"And nothing else? Like something I can do on the side?" Li-An was starting to worry about boredom. Samantha stared at her with the same curious look, but soon regained her composure.

"Not for the first couple months. It all depends on how you react though. Some take as long as six months to feel any change, others one to two. A very few have no reaction to the pills at all. Anyway, you'll find out yourself soon." Samantha waved her left hand in the air dismissively and went about inspecting the room with her clipboard in hand to ensure all was in order.

"You'll rest for today. Tomorrow, someone will come and bring you to meet Professor Evans. Around here we sometimes call him Professor FAME, because his given name is Fabian Angus Mark Evans. It's what you get when you put together the initials. You'll hear us say that, but don't call him that yourself. 10 am sharp, so be ready when they come for you. Read this carefully before you meet him tomorrow." Li-An stretched her right arm to receive the handout from Samantha, who delivered it with a snapping motion and then strutted out of the room with what Li-An now thought was a conceited gait. She had a strange feeling she'd met Samantha somewhere before.

Li-An leafed through the papers, not intending to pay much attention. Most were minor details. The timing of breakfast, lunch, and dinner. All to be served in the same restaurant. There were also instructions to behave like a normal human being and not a medical test subject when not in one's room. Yada yada. Then on page 15 Li-An caught an unusual clause: a promise to account professionally for her lost time as a human subject in a medical trial. She went out to the terrace, sat down on the reclining deck chair, and carefully studied the choice of words and phrasing.

Clause 37: Upon completion of the trials, the subject will be awarded a credential (e.g. educational degree, professional certification, etc.) of his or her own choice in cooperation with the responsible agency or institution of the Republic of Kramen. Upon issuance of the credential, the subject may use this for job search purposes, in order to account for the time spent in the trial. The subject is under no circumstances to divulge that they were a human subject in this trial, either in writing or orally, once they have completed the project, lest this credential be revoked, and other dire consequences follow.

In other words, the project was so secretive that they were going to tailor a cover story for each human subject to account for the two-year gap in their resumes. Not only would her looks improve, Li-An realized, but the time spent at Sentacruz would not come at the expense of a career. Ethically dubious, perhaps, but if the government was willing to go this far, it meant that the project was important, and keeping it secret trumped all other considerations. Never mind the last four words "other dire consequences follow", whatever they meant. Feeling that she had more to gain than lose, Li-An looked around for the hotel pen and signed on the agreement form appended to the documents.

It was the following morning. A knock on her door. Li-An checked the clock and saw that it was precisely 10 am. She opened the door and standing in front of her was Samantha Tan. But hadn't Samantha told her someone else was going to pick her up?

"Samantha!" Li-An puckered her eyebrows.

"Good morning, Li-An. I'm actually Clarissa. Samantha's my twin sister. I'm here to bring you to meet our research leader, Professor Evans. He's expecting you. By the way, we only do English names here, so you'll be called Julianne from now on."

Li-An was fazed. Not so much by the appearance of an identical twin, but that Clarissa somehow knew that she'd also called herself Julianne back in school. She'd not written that on her application.

They walked down a series of corridors, then turned right to face what looked like the door to another hotel room. But when Clarissa tapped the card on the sensor next to it, the door opened to reveal a lift. She pushed the button for the third sub-basement and when the lift door opened again, Li-An found herself in a large, dimly-lit hall without windows, but filled with lab equipment. It was such an unlikely space to be buried deep under a resort hotel. As her eyes were still adjusting to the light level, a man entered through a door located at the far end, accompanied by a spotlight aiming at his feet. Professor FAME, she reckoned. As he walked towards Li-An, the professor spread his arms wide and his face brightened into a broad grin. But Li-An felt more nervous than welcomed.

"Welcome to The Lab of Possibilities! And you are one of the chosen few!" This must have been the professor's stock greeting because Li-An noticed through the dimness that Clarissa was rolling her eyes.

Evans was not dressed in any sort of professorial fashion. Bell-bottoms half-hid a pair of heavyweight leather boots – which made a distinctive clip-clop sound when he walked towards Li-An – and his top was a frilly white shirt with sleeves that flared at the elbow. His neck was wrapped in a yellow polka-dotted bow tie. When he talked, Li-An noticed that the sides of his mouth seemed to crack. She could tell that his face was hidden under a cakey layer of foundation, making him look almost artificial. The cracks were lines formed by the congealed powder which creased into deep wrinkles whenever the professor smiled. This helped explain the faint lighting in the room, she thought, and the spotlight focusing on his feet instead of the face, though she could still make out his facial expressions. Li-An was instantly curious about this man.

"What's your name again? Julianne?" Evans looked to Clarissa, who nodded her head.

"Yes, that's right. Well, Julianne, let me give you an explanation of what we do here. I'm the research leader in this elaborate laboratory and I'm working to create a better strain of the human species, no less." The professor put his right arm around Li-An's shoulder and began to lead her around the room. The spotlight religiously followed Evans' footsteps, and froze without delay if he stopped to explain something. Li-An looked around her, hoping to locate a control room - a source for the beam but couldn't make one out. It was as though the spotlight was an extension of the professor himself.

". . . one that is less susceptible to aging. You see all these cell specimens here? If you look at them under the microscope, you'll see an amazing transformation taking place. Come, see for yourself." Evans' excitement escalated as he talked. He brought her to a long row of microscopes on desk tops arranged in a big concentric circle. There were dozens of them. Evans invited Li-An to peer through the microscopes, one at a time, as he explained his research at length. Without much of a science background, Li-An couldn't make heads nor tails of what she saw, or what he was talking about, and soon became bored.

"I know what you're thinking. Nothing special, right?" said the professor, correctly reading her mind. "It looks like regular cell division." He was talking to her as though she were a fellow microbiologist.

"But with some meddling. . ." Evans fluttered the fingers of one hand to evoke an impossibly complicated process he was not going to explain. "We're actually altering the genetic structure." The professor shot Li An a sly look. She did her best to look impressed.

"Project X Inverted. That's what we call it!" Li-An knew that X was the shape associated with chromosomes, though in actual fact they looked nothing like that alphabetic character.

"Why inverted?" Li-An was happy to have a question to ask.

"So this is my new baby!" said the professor, ignoring Li-An's question, and gesturing to one of the slides, or perhaps all of them. She figured his "baby" was the project.

"But that's not the only thing I do. You've met Samantha as well as Clarissa, no?"

"Yes." replied Li-An.

"Well, they're not really twins. One of them is a clone. The world's very first human clone." Evans pointed to Clarissa as he spoke. "And the only one that will probably ever exist in your lifetime." "It's the *ethicists*" he said, slurring the word to show his disapproval. "I came here to escape them, but they're even in Kramen now. And China, and everywhere else. The first human clones would have given your country so much prestige, but I'm forbidden to announce or publish it." He paused, as though reconsidering what he'd just said. "And now you are too."

"But Project X Inverted is different, and better. The government is fully behind me on this. You simply won't believe what this little pill can do." Evans picked up with a tweezer what looked like a regular pill. White and oblong-shaped. She figured this was the pill Samantha mentioned. The one she was here to take.

"If this works, the rest of the world will scramble for it. And your country will be rolling in dough . . . and I'll be famous!" laughed the professor heartily. "That's why they tease me with the nickname. Anyway . . ." Just as Li-An thought she was about to get an explanation of the drug she'd be taking for the next two years, the Professor suddenly seemed to lose interest in her. He turned in the direction of the door, and unexpectedly strode out of the room with only a slight wave of the hand to signal that the meeting was finished. The spotlight vanished along with him. Clarissa waited for the door to completely shut.

"Let's go. The performance is over. Don't worry, I'll explain everything later," she said.

Li-An, whose eyes were just getting used to the dim lighting, now saw that the walls and floor were painted with a pattern of tightly-spaced squiggly lines expanding out in orderly fashion from a circle she was standing in. It had an almost dizzying effect. The word "trippy" came to mind. The professor seemed to have strong feelings for the fashion and design of the nineteen sixties. Down here it was an entirely different world from the one above their heads, with the peacocks and the frangipani trees. How, she wondered, was she to survive among these strange people for the next two years.

3 LETSCHAT

Year: 2016. Li-An's age: 38 (but only days away from 39)

It was just past midnight on Christmas. Li-An was at Kramen International Airport waiting to board. As usual, mainland Chinese tourists had already formed a long seamless queue facing the jet bridge. Li-An looked past the queue and saw some elderly and middle-aged Chinese waiting to fill their water bottles at the cooler stand. There were left-behind traces of oversoaked tea leaves laying limp and lifeless in the basin, and loud exchanges in local dialects which Li-An could hardly make out. Then the sound system in the holding area crackled, signalling it was time to board. Li-An had bought the BoardMeFirst priority pass – the only one purchased for that flight – so had access to the plane before anybody else.

"15F, 15F, 15F......" A sleepy Li-An finally found her seat and tossed her North Face duffel bag into the overhead compartment. The bag had long served to carry her important Chinese research documents from the early Communist period and Li-An always felt it to be a heavy burden. But tonight, it was filled only with light winter wear and lifting the bag over her head became an effortless task.

15F. The aisle seat in the middle column on the right-hand side. She always requested an aisle seat at the check-in counter. Li-An knew deep down it was her way of rebelling against the man – her first boyfriend - who'd told her to always ask for a window seat. But sitting by the aisle had increasingly grown on her. No need to say a word to the person to her left or right if she had to go to the restroom. She hoped no one would sit next to her on this trip, but as soon as she settled down passengers began pressing into the aisles. A man stopped in the aisle just beside her arm, his eyes switching quickly between his boarding pass and the seat numbers. He'd likely overshot. Due to parallax error, Li-An had often mistaken her seat for the one in front or back. She dared a quick upward glance. Medium-height. Early forties. Rugged but on the whole good-looking. Li-An could tell from underneath the white t-shirt that the man had spent time in the gym. She thought he looked tired, but after all it was past midnight.

"Could you please let me through?" the man politely turned to Li-An. She nodded and shifted slightly to the right.

As he awkwardly shuffled past, Li-An recorded more details. He was wearing steely blue sweatpants with matching Li-Ning running shoes. He pulled out his cellphone, sat at the seat next to hers, keyed in a few Chinese characters on LetsChat, and switched the phone off. Someone in the world cared that he was about to take off.

Li-An took out a novel from her pocket book. She'd gotten it at the airport bookstore on her way to the boarding gate. Li-An always relished long-distance travel for the opportunity to spend hours in the world made from words. She'd even compiled a to-buy list of current books, and took pleasure in shopping for them at the airport bookstore. Purchasing them at the airport just before takeoff made them seem more connected to the experience of the flight. But after a minute or so, she sensed the man's stare – first at the book, then her, then the book. Feeling his stare, she read defiantly on.

The plane was filling up, and, like her immediate neighbor, everyone around her was busy typing their final messages on LetsChat. This Chinese platform worked like most social media apps around the world. Users could post photos, constantly update their life in real time and eagerly await the number of "likes" they'd receive in the form of a heart-shaped icon, or best of all a praiseful comment. But LetsChat was even more useful than foreign platforms, because it allowed one to pay bills, hail a taxi, and even give out red packets on festive days. There was no longer a need to carry cash around China, just a smartphone with an active LetsChat account linked to one's bank balance. In the subway train, over meals, just before take-off, or simply idling around, LetsChat was like a tiny treadmill for Chinese fingers, endlessly scrolling up and down the screen. "Lai, Jia Ge Lexin Ba" had become the standard parting phrase in China. "Come, let's add each other on LetsChat". As a foreigner, Li-An had not made LetsChat into an addiction, but it was useful.

Li-An often wondered why the English translation for LetsChat was not Happy Letter since happy was the more accurate translation for *le*, while *xin* actually meant letter. One thing about it wasn't very happy though: the Chinese government was reading all these messages, or at least government computers were. Though it didn't seem to matter to anyone she knew.

The plane took off and the cabin lights dimmed. Li-An spent a couple hours reading her novel before her eyes grew heavy and she closed the book hoping to sleep. And she did doze for a while. When she opened her eyes, Li-An noticed the aisle seat at the other end of the row was now empty. She then looked intently at her neighbor, now dozing, hoping he'd sense her stare. He did, and his eyes opened.

"Would you mind moving over one seat? I'd like to lie down." The man obliged. Li-An lifted the armrest to take the extra space. She then fell on her right side, facing the back of the seats in front of her. There was no room for her legs and she felt the stretch on her left waist as she let her feet hang over the seat. But she slept for a while. Twenty-minutes later, she was woken up by a light thump on her upper body. She opened her eyes and saw that the man had taken off his winter jacket and draped it over her. She sat up to return him the jacket.

"No, take it. It's cold. You're wearing too little." His eyes were only half-opened.

He was right. Li-An indeed felt cold, wearing only Uniqlo's Heattech thermal wear. She was thinking of bringing her winter jacket down when the man offered her his. She actually felt warmer with the extra layer and slept soundly for the rest of the flight.

When she woke it was six-thirty in the morning, Beijing time. One more hour before touch down. Being a budget flight, the airline was not about to serve breakfast nor give out fancy amenities. She still had the winter jacket. Li-An looked over to her left and saw that the man was still sleeping. She ran her fingers through her hair to make sure every strand was in place, then reached forward and gently placed the jacket over its owner. He immediately opened his eyes. She'd turned her body 90 degrees so that they made eye contact for the first time. "Xie Xie Ah." "Thank you," she said, and flashed him a smile. By ending her sentence with "ah", Li-An made her voice sound even more feminine. She returned to her original aisle seat, and buckled up to prepare for landing. He stretched his legs and arms to wake himself up, put the jacket back on, and took out his cellphone. Her gestures seemed to have had an effect on him, as he returned to his original seat, and she could sense him stealing glances in her direction. The plane was in mid-descent.

"You are in your twenties?" he suddenly asked. Li-An gave him a sheepish nod.

"Where are you from?"

"Kramen Island. . . Ah! Snow!" Li-An looked past the man out the plane window, her body shifting slightly to directly face the window diagonally on her far left. She was trying to avert questions she wasn't comfortable answering, like her real age.

"So, you like snow?" The man involuntarily followed Li-An's gaze.

"It's just there's none where I come from, and when I'm in China it's usually down south. Not up this far."

"What do you do?" The man asked.

"I'm a researcher. You?"

"I work for a real estate developer. My company has a project off the coast of Jiamen Dao", he said, using the Chinese term for Kramen Island. "I spent two days there and one day in your city."

"My country's expensive, no?" The man quietly nodded and Li-An couldn't tell if he was agreeing with her, or she'd inadvertently insulted him. The exchange rate between Kramen Island and China was one Kramen dollar to five Chinese yuan, roughly speaking.

"Which part of China are you from?" she asked

"Yan'an."

"Where Chairman Mao and his PLA were based."

"Oh, you know." The man sounded impressed.

"Of course, I'm a historian."

Just then the plane landed. The man switched on his phone. Li-An saw his screen wallpaper was a selfie of him kissing a girl on her lips.

"Ni You Lexin Ma? "Do you have LetsChat?" The man brought his cellphone closer to Li-An. A gesture to either scan her QR code or just signal he wanted her ID or contact number.

"I'm not using a local SIM card, so can't use my phone right now. But you can add me first," she said. The man keyed in Li-An's ID number.

"What's your name?"

"Li-An. And yours?"

"Bai Xiang. And by the way, you're not wearing enough. It's cold outside. You need to wear more." Translated to English, the characters in the man's name spelled 'White Fortune'.

"I know. What I'm wearing is only the first layer. I've thicker ones up there." Li-An pointed to the overhead compartment.

Even before the plane came to a full stop, the Chinese passengers began unfastening their seat belts and reaching for their stuff in the overhead compartment. The Krameans predictably remained seated until the seatbelt sign was turned off.

The beep finally came. Li-An stood up, placed her duffel bag on her seat, took out her passport, and joined the line of passengers at the aisle. The man moved to stand at Li-An's seat. She was checking to see if the details on her disembarkation card were correctly filled out when he spoke to her again.

"May I take a look at your passport?" Seeing that he'd already stretched out his palm, Li-An unwillingly obliged. He looked intently at the cover. "K-R-A-M-E-N." The man sounded awkward spelling out the Latin script. "This must be the English for Jiamen Dao, no?" He asked. This signaled Li-An that he wasn't well-educated, but she made sure not to register it on her face.

She nodded, all the while hoping he wouldn't flip over the cover and see her real birthdate. To her relief he didn't, but politely returned it.

"Merry Christmas and Happy New Year," Li-An said with a smile.

"Same to you," he replied. As the line began to move, Li-An turned and walked away.

"That was too close," she thought, and made a mental note never to share her passport with strangers again. The difference between her appearance and her birthdate was bound to raise questions she was tired of answering. And in any case, she liked that younger strangers took her to be one of them. She heaved a sigh of relief and headed for immigration.

After clearing customs, Li-An spotted a couple rows of chairs at the baggage claim area, and walked in that direction. She put down her duffel bag, unzipped it, and put on her black waterproof pants lined with thick fleece, followed by her favorite ash grey fluffy scarf, and the stylish metallic gold down coat she'd bought a week ago for half the original price. She took out her phone, replaced her Kramen sim card with the local one, and saw that the man from the plane had indeed added her on LetsChat. "No harm," she thought, adding him back. Li-An then went to the baggage carousel to pick up her suitcase, which she'd already sighted from a distance. "He must have left," she thought, glancing around despite herself. Li-An recalled on the plane seeing the man holding only a carton of cigarettes sealed in the Security Tamper Evident Bag. Other than that, he had nothing. No carry-ons. Neither did she see him at the baggage claim area. "Odd," she thought. But it was none of her business if he hadn't changed his clothes for three days. She proceeded to the exit, her right hand lightly pushing her four-wheeled suitcase.

This wasn't the first time Li-An had arrived at Tianjin Binhai International Airport. Budget airlines preferred to use the airports of tier two cities like Tianjin. Beijing was only another 35 minutes via the high-speed train. And for a first-class train seat, Li-An had to pay only 11 US dollars. The total sum of airfare and train tickets was half of what she'd have to fork out to fly straight to Beijing from Kramen. A good deal. While a PhD student, Li-An had learnt to maximize the use of her research funding by flying on budget airlines and staying in cheap youth hostels. Even if that meant sharing a room with four – sometimes up to nine – female strangers. Males too, if the hostel only had mixed dormitories. And putting up with inconsiderate roommates who either snored too loudly at night, or interrupted her sleep if they returned late. Hostel-stayers were mostly tourists, and all the doors at Chinese youth hostels operated on a card system which made a sound when activated. Li-An wrote practically her entire dissertation in these surroundings, under the small, dim lights attached to hostel beds. But not for this trip. She was determined to splurge and pamper herself.

Li-An stopped to get her bearings at the arrival hall. In front of her a signboard with an arrow pointing upward and a symbol for the subway train. Straight ahead. Li-An started the long walk in that direction, picking up speed with each step.

She spotted the man from the plane as she walked past a row of counters, just as he in turn spotted her. They turned to face each other.

"Oh, hi again. You're all layered up" he said.

"Yes, what are you doing?" she said.

"I just returned the wi-fi router to the counter." Li-An caught the eye of another man looking at her from a distance. "He's my colleague," said the man from the plane, following her gaze.

"I've already added you on LetsChat," he said.

She was about to say "I know", when he abruptly said "I'll talk to you later" and started walking back to his colleague. It was obvious to her that he'd wanted to show his colleague she wasn't anyone who mattered to him.

Li-An turned and walked a few more steps before taking the escalator down to the subway in the basement.

She took the train to the "Radio and TV Tower" station.

As soon as she got off the train and out of the exit, Li-An spotted a cab. She waved for the driver's attention, then hopped in.

On her way to the hotel, the man kept texting her.

26th December 2016, 9.15 am

"Nin Hao!" The man added a smiley face with a wink and tongue sticking out. He had used the honorific expression for "you" (nin). Together Nin Hao meant hello, but more respectful.

"Have you reached your hotel?" (red-faced icon with a droplet of sweat on the right-side of head, facial features twitching to the left indicating concern)

"I'm in a taxi," Li-An wrote back, hoping to stop the messages, which were distracting her from interacting with the driver.

"We're already at Tianjin station and you still haven't arrived at your destination yet?"

Li-An ignored his message.

When Li-An gave the driver the booking reservation she'd made through sleepeasy.com, he told her upfront that he'd never heard of the hotel. Snow was starting to fall. Reluctant to alight and brave the weather, Li-An pleaded with the driver and promised to add 20 yuan to the price on the meter if he'd try. He knew the neighborhood at least. After they got there, he spent the next ten minutes asking directions from people walking on the streets. Finally, one said "Just further down where the overhead bridge is." Within 5 minutes, Li-An was at the entrance of Fraser Place Tianjin. Entering the lobby, she was greeted by a female concierge in heavily accented English.

"My taxi driver wasn't sure how to get to here. Is the hotel new?" asked Li-An.

"Yes, we're barely a year old. And nowhere near a subway station, which makes it hard to give them directions. I'm sorry." The concierge turned her gaze back to the computer screen. There was a big Christmas tree in the lobby, and the hotel was playing jazz versions of carols, despite the Chinese government's discouragement of what it called a foreign holiday.

"Thank you for waiting. Here's your room card. We're upgrading you to a family suite. It's located on the twenty-fifth floor. Just turn left and you'll see the lift. Please enjoy your stay."

It was an impressive two-bedroom apartment, over 100 square meters by the look of it. The floor was laminated to imitate real solid wood, and there was a kitchenette equipped (though barely so) with Western fittings for an international look. The carpeted living room alone was the size of the studio apartment Li-An rented in a modest neighborhood of Kramen Island. She went to check both bedrooms. The master bedroom lay at the end of the hallway. A large rectangle, somewhere between 36 and 40 square meters. It even had its own bathtub: a rare luxury in Kramen, where space was at such a premium. Shampoo, conditioner, body wash, body lotion. The amenities were labeled in impeccable English, and stressed their use of natural ingredients. The king-sized bed had neatly tucked-in corners. Its four pillows had a puffed-up look, but stood in a too-stern fashion against the headstand, like a line of soldiers. There was a dressing table against the wall, and a foreign-branded

42-inch LED TV. With the door closed, the master bedroom felt absolutely private and self-contained. The other bedroom was much smaller by comparison. Two single beds and a wardrobe. Tight spacing. Enough to make one feel constricted moving between them.

The second bathroom, located across the corridor, only had a shower. "Good! He can sleep in this room," she thought, referring to her fiancé. She pulled her cellphone from her coat pocket, went onto LetsChat, and searched for him on the messaging page. Hui. The Chinese character for Grey. Li-An sometimes wondered if the reason why her fiancé used this and not his real name was because his hair was increasingly turning that color.

"I just arrived in Tianjin," wrote Li-An.

Li-An also noticed the text from the man on the airplane. Until she messaged her fiancé, the man had appeared at the top of her LetsChat page, but was now pushed to second place. She noticed the surname of the man from the plane and her fiancé's LetsChat alias formed a nice color contrast: White and Grey.

Li-An felt like taking a shower and wheeled her suitcase to the master bedroom. She took out her toiletry kit. A black, masculine zipper bag she'd taken from one of her previous dates.

26th December 2016, 10.23 am

"Drink some warm water. It's almost lunch time." Li-An had just finished her shower and was running the bath when White began texting again.

"You seem thoughtful. I'm envious of your girlfriend," she wrote back facetiously.

"It's a pleasure to meet you. How long are you staying in China?" White began his sentence with a 'chuckle' icon, which was his non-answer to Li-An's mention of his girlfriend.

"Just one day in Beijing . . . but I'm on a work mission," she lied. "Do you listen to Beijing punk rock?"

"You like that stuff?"

"Yes," she lied. Li-An wanted to create things which they did not have in common. She figured he wouldn't like punk rock any more than she did. She'd just read an article about the punk scene in Beijing so it was the first dissonant thing that came to mind.

"Li-An, how long are you staying in China?" White asked a second time.

"Two weeks, but soon I leave for Harbin." Why was she even telling him this, she thought?

"It's fate that we met. The rest of my team had sat together, except for me." (a yellow-faced icon with eyebrows lifted in an inverted V shape, two straight lines for the eyes and one droplet of sweat on the right. The cheeks were colored red to indicate, what, embarrassment?)

26th December 2016, 10. 30 am

"And that's how I have the opportunity to know you," he continued.

26th December 2016, 10.31 am

"For which I'm very happy."

26th December 2016, 10.36 am

"I also want to tell you a secret. I've never had a foreign friend." (eyes big and round with both irises looking to the right. The two eyebrows drawn above the head like two insect feelers. One finger placed on the lips to reinforce secrecy.)

Li-An's cellphone kept sounding like a doorbell. White had sent so many messages, sprinkled with emoticons, that she couldn't keep up. She couldn't decide if she was more irritated or flattered.

"My ancestors were originally from Guangdong, so I'm half a mainlander," she wrote back. It was a hint to the man that she was actually not that 'foreign', or exotic.

"Have you eaten?"

"No, I'm heading out soon for a meeting," she lied again.

"But first, you should eat something. Tianjin is dry. Drink more water."

"You sound just like a Shanghainese. I bet you cook for your girlfriend too."

"Is that so? These are basic manners. I'm sorry, but I only know how to fry eggs." (a wide grin, teeth showing with both eyes and eyebrows curving in like an inverted U-shape.)

Li-An knew the Chinese saying that Shanghainese men made good husbands, comparatively speaking. They were supposed to be able to cook and do all the household chores. The bath was ready. Li-An searched for her Skross world travel adaptor, and plugged it into the wall. After putting her cellphone on the charger, she quickly dashed for the bathroom.

Soaking in the bathtub, the phone beeped again in the other room. She cursed herself for not turning the sound down.

Li-An decided it was enough. She got out of the bathtub, wrapped herself in a towel, half-dripping as she tiptoed to the bedside table, then picked up and switched off her phone. She saw that the new message was actually from her fiancé, but decided she'd deal with it later. She'd change the notification sound once she was done with her bath. Contrary to what she'd told the man, Li-An had no plans to leave the hotel room. She only wanted to order room service, sleep off her fatigue from last night's plane ride, and catch up on Chinese TV programs. Finishing her bath, Li-An switched her phone back on to read her fiancé's message. He'd bought an air ticket to Tianjin and would arrive late that night. Li-An acknowledged his message with "en", Chinese for "yes" or "ok", pressed "Me" to go into "settings" and under "notifications" selected the sound of bubbles. She soon fell asleep.

By the time Li-An woke, it was dark outside. She ordered a club sandwich through room service. As she was eating, Li-An remembered the man on the plane. White. She picked up her phone lying next to her on the dinner table, went into his profile page and started scrolling down to look at his earlier postings. The most recent were of his visit to Kramen and the neighboring artificial island of Forest Paradise, under construction by a Chinese developer. The top entry showed familiar Kramen tourist sites. Chinatown and the just-built billion-dollar garden that looked like a set from a sci-fi movie, designed to maintain Kramen Island as a top Asian tourist destination. Another picture showed the man holding his palm up. He'd positioned himself so that water spurting out from the island's most iconic statue – a lion with the tail of a fish, and located across the river from where he was posing – seemed to land right onto his palm. A typical, cheesy, tourist pose. A LetsChat friend of Li-An's visiting Kramen Island months before had posed so that the water seemed to spray into his mouth. In a separate posting, the man was pictured astride a jet ski, likely at Forest Paradise. He'd even gotten a colleague to shoot a 10-second video of him in action. The sleeveless t-shirt revealed a broad, beefy shoulder. So the man had brought more than one set of clothes.

Forest Paradise, the huge Chinese-managed development project just off the Kramen coast, was constantly in the newspapers and on TV, although no one Li-An knew had traveled there. So, the man was telling the truth. He was working for China's best performing real estate developer: Huamanyuan (Flower Blossom Garden).

26th December 2016, 8.25 pm

"Li-An, what're you doing?" It was White again.

26th December 2016, 8.26 pm

"I'm looking at your postings," she replied.
"What else are you doing?" he asked.
"Nothing."
"How's the weather?"
"Not bad. Not as cold as I'd expected."
"Still, the air is smoggy. Best to stay indoors."
"You're thoughtful, giving all this advice." Li-An used the Chinese "ti tie nan" (thoughtful man).
"Will you be in Beijing for the New Year?" he asked.
"Yes. But don't you have to keep your girlfriend company?"
"Call me." White wrote down his number in the next message.
"You haven't answered me. Your girlfriend."
"No, not at all."
"Then, let's meet the day after New Year. On the second." Li-An began her message with a yellow-faced emoticon stifling a laugh. Left hand was placed over the mouth with eyes curved in an inverted U-shape. She was surprised by the boldness of her own message. It was an invitation for a date.

The man responded with a thumbs-up.

Li-An spent the rest of the night researching about Forest Paradise. She even imagined living there in a high apartment with a balcony, and just watching Kramen in the distance, but never going back. Standing on the balcony next to her, despite her best efforts to edit her imagination, was White, the man from the airplane.

4 THE DATE

It was past midnight. Li-An was woken by a voice call on LetsChat. Grey, her fiancé, had arrived at Fraser Place Tianjin.

"So you're here." Li-An yawned while answering the call.

"Yes, I'm at the lobby," he replied.

Li-An got out of bed, changed into her black thermal wear, put on her sweater and winter boots, and took the lift down to where he was waiting.

"Hi." She greeted him in a neutral tone.

"Sorry to be so late," he apologized, matching her inflection.

"How long will you be here?" she asked, pressing the lift button.

"Just one day. Tomorrow. I've class the following day."

Behind them the lift made a dinging sound. Instinctively they both turned to face it, Li-An entering first. An awkward silence. It was so late that nobody else was about, so the lift rocketed them up to Li-An's 25th floor suite without stopping.

"Wow! This is huge!" he exclaimed as she ushered him in, seizing on the talking point of the room to change the mood.

"How much did you pay for this?" he asked.

"A little less than 3000 yuan for five nights. A good deal huh? Why don't you go and shower? I'll be in my room." Li-An showed him his room before returning to hers.

She changed into her pajamas, placed the pillows upright and propped herself up with them as she switched the TV on. Ten minutes later, he entered her room through the door she'd left open, and went to sit on the stool next to the dressing table opposite the bed. Li-An switched the TV off.

"You flew all the way here from Hangzhou only for one day?" she asked.

"Well, it's been a while since we met. I suppose we have things to talk about. What's your plan for tomorrow?" He looked calm and composed. He reminded her of the way he'd behaved when they first met, but almost never since the engagement. Maybe it'd been a long day and he was too exhausted to act up. Or maybe her dimming the lights in her room softened his mood. Or maybe her coldness to him these past six months had made him self-reflective. It didn't matter, she thought, as long as it lasted.

"But the amount you must have spent on the air-ticket," she remarked.

"No, it's not a lot of money. Anyway, it's late. We should sleep and talk tomorrow. I know we're both tired. Goodnight." And with that he left the room.

The next morning, they had breakfast at the hotel restaurant. It was included in the room fee. As usual, Li-An started with a plate of salad and a piece of toast. Western selection. Grey opted for the typical Chinese breakfast. Porridge topped with pickles, a few crumbs of the salted egg, and fried anchovies. His main course was a plate of fried noodles surrounded by various dim-sumy things. Shao Mai: pork wrapped in a thin egg flour sheet. Xia Jiao: shrimp held in a translucent white pocket with neatly folded edges on one side. And two barbecue pork buns. A healthy appetite for someone with a small frame. Li-An loved Chinese food as well, just not for breakfast.

But there was at least one thing both she and her fiancé had in common. Both preferred tea to coffee. She stopped drinking coffee after an incident more than a decade before, at Sentacruz. She'd ordered an espresso shot at the resort's café and was rendered immobile half an hour later. Likely because of some interaction with the Xter pills. Although she recovered the next day, Li-An never drank coffee again. She figured it was a small sacrifice given how the pills transformed her. But it did make her wonder what other side effects she might encounter without warning. After all, she was their guinea pig.

"So why did you come to the mainland all of a sudden?" asked Grey. Li-An was quietly sipping her tea and staring blankly out the window at the glistening snow – it was a bright, clear morning. A woman had unleashed her two dogs and they were chasing after each other. One was a husky and its white fur blended with the snow on the ground. Li-An was following the dogs' movements at the back of her mind. The scene let her pause for a moment before answering him.

"I just want to take a break, that's all. Now that I've completed my PhD, I want to see China from a different angle. As a tourist." She was looking at her tea and rubbing the rim of the teacup with her right index finger as she spoke.

"Why China?" he asked with detective sharpness.

"Why not?" Li-An sounded agitated and her fiancé took the cue. She wouldn't tell him she was on her way to a holiday alone in Harbin. It was meant as a gift to herself.

"Shall we go explore Tianjin after breakfast?" he asked. Li-An nodded. It was a way to fill their time without too much talk.

"You look like you're all dressed up for Siberia." They'd gone back to their room after breakfast to put on more clothing before heading out. Now Li-An was all warm and snug in the black waterproof pants with an extra inner fleece lining which she'd bought especially for Harbin. When she slipped into her fake UGG winter boots and lifted the hood – which came with a fake fur trimming to cover her head - she could easily pass for an Eskimo. "Shall we go?" she said, not responding to Grey's Siberia comment. It was too on-the-spot. Harbin was just across the border from Russia.

They spent three hours visiting shops, each in their own world but occasionally chatting about things they discovered. Li-An was not in a buying mood, and deflected all his attempts to buy things for her. She would turn 39 in a couple of days, but Li-An did not want any gifts from him. She could tell it frustrated Grey, this "no thank you" mode when he wanted to be generous; when he thought some heroic purchase, like an expensive hand-bag, would in one stroke set things right.

When they returned to the hotel Li-An was sweating so much – the outfit was in the end too warm for Tianjin – that she had to shower. Forty-five minutes later, she came out of her room with only a bathrobe on. He was cracking melon seeds at the dining table. Li-An went to sit on the couch, facing him.

"Now that you've completed your degree, what do you plan to do next?" he followed the question with a smile.

"What do you mean?" asked Li-An, feigning ignorance. She knew exactly what he meant. Was she ready to marry him?

"Well, do you plan to look for a job here or back home in Kramen Island?"

"The lights here are too bright. Let's talk in my bedroom," she said. Li-An left the couch and headed for her room. She was already lying on the bed when he entered. "May I lie next to you?" he asked.

"Alright," she answered. He laid down on her right. A moment of silence. Slowly, he stretched out his right hand and carefully placed it just below her breasts. With her left hand, Li-An grabbed hold of her bathrobe collar, yet at the same time, she felt excited. She realized she was secretly craving his touch.

"You've been ignoring me all this while. Are you breaking up with me?" he asked.

"I don't know," Li-An replied in a soft, timid voice.

"I miss you a lot." He leaned closer to her, his lips touching her neck. She could hear the sound of his breath. Worried that he might unloosen her belt, Li-An shifted slightly to the left. Still, she was feeling excited despite herself.

"Why did you ignore me?" he murmured. "You don't want me anymore?" He kissed her right cheek.

Li-An didn't reveal her arousal. Rather, she only showed the side of herself that was scared. She was still grabbing tightly onto the bathrobe collar.

"It's been a while. I'm not sure about this," she said as she curled up like a fetus.

"And I'm on my period. It's ending soon. But still . . ." Li-An was surprised by her ambiguity. Why not make it definite? Why even entertain the idea of sex from a man who'd been so rough to her, physically and emotionally?

"I'll put a towel underneath." Grey got out of bed and went into the bathroom. Seconds later he emerged with a white body towel.

Li-An had by now removed her thick bathrobe. She lifted her bum while he neatly spread the towel underneath her.

"Where's your condom?" she said. He hadn't placed a condom on the side table which was his usual habit.

"I didn't bring. It's ok. I don't need it. I just want to touch you."

Grey lightly caressed her breasts. First the left, then the right. "I miss them." He suckled Li-An gently, not with his usual roughness. She let out a little moan of pleasure. He then ran his right hand along Li-An's body and finally down to her vagina. She spread her legs while he brushed her clitoris using his fingertips. Lightly at first, then picking up speed to a vibrating momentum so that eventually she came. As he withdrew his fingers, Li-An turned away from him to lie on her left. Slowly, she closed her eyes and drifted off to sleep.

She woke up half an hour later, and turned to see him all dressed. He was sitting upright next to her and checking his LetsChat messages.

"I'm leaving for the airport in an hour." Grey stopped his messaging and placed his cellphone on the side table to his right. He then turned to hold Li-An in his arms. Li-An refused to move. Sensing her resistance, he retracted his hand.

"What are we now? Are we on or off?" Li-An didn't answer.

"It's natural for couples to fight and squabble. But giving me short little answers on LetsChat. Or none at all. For six months! It's too extreme. Can't we just talk it through?"

"He hasn't really changed." Li-An thought to herself. She was tempted to remind him of his own extreme behavior earlier that year but was afraid of provoking him. He wasn't one to listen.

"Let's start the new year afresh, shall we?" he asked. Li-An nodded and even managed to smile as she saw him to the door. But soon after she closed it, she let out a sigh. "Is that it?" she asked herself. "Is this my fate?" She was a human subject in a clinical trial, Li-An reminded herself. And so was her fiancé, though he didn't know it. She'd made her decision, or they'd made it for her. OK, they'd all made it together. But Li-An couldn't turn back now, because she'd run out the clock. There simply wasn't any more time.

Li-An arrived in Beijing on New Year's Eve, and checked into the Park Plaza hotel. Unlike Fraser Place Tianjin, the hotel didn't offer an upgrade but gave exactly what she'd paid for: a regular room which they nonetheless called "deluxe". But it was the location that Li-An wanted. Wangfujing. Beijing's shopping district. Li-An hadn't anticipated meeting a man on a plane and having a date, so none of the clothes she'd packed were suitable. She needed to go shopping, and the hotel location was perfect. As soon as she checked into her room, Li-An grabbed her backpack and left for the nearby shops. She remembered a boutique specializing in cheongsam when she'd come to Beijing three years before. Li-An loved cheongsam, or qipao as they were also called, because they showed off her curves. The modern ones anyway. As an historian, she knew they were never so tight-fitting traditionally. She returned to the mall where she'd last seen it, but the boutique was gone, like so many others in the age of e-shopping.

In the end, she settled for a contemporary-style dress. The fabric from the chest down was made of a nice heavy material imprinted with regular-spaced horizontal lines but interrupted by vertical stripes of varying thickness. A contrast to the light, transparent long-sleeved black chiffon from the shoulder up. The dress matched Li-An's black UGG imitation boots, so she didn't have to buy a new pair.

1ˢᵗ January 2017, 9.39 pm

"Happy New Year!" wrote Li-An to White. She added graphics of two popped holiday crackers for a festive effect.

"Same to you. You are spending the New Year in China alone. I wish you happiness." White ended his text with a smiley making two peace signs, one on each side of the face. Did he even remember their date? Li-An told herself to assume that he did.

"I'm staying at the Park Plaza Hotel. It's on Wangfujing. Shall we meet somewhere near for dinner?

"Sure."

"See ya tomorrow." Li-An signed off with a regular smiling emoticon.

"Ok," he replied.

It wasn't clear to Li-An if she wanted the date. Upon returning from the shopping trip, she simply threw the bag holding the newly-bought dress to one corner rather than taking it out and hanging it up, as she usually would. She kept reminding herself that he was just a nice distraction. White was a good-looking Chinese from the north. A refreshing change from her fiancé, who was a short, older Southerner. She told herself the dinner would be a one-off thing, since she didn't plan on coming back to the mainland until her marriage, later that year. So when the next day came, still with no news from White past noontime, Li-An didn't see a reason to text him. Maybe he wasn't coming after all.

2nd January 2017, 2.11 pm

"Li-An, when shall we meet?" White's message appeared on her phone after lunch.

"5pm at Wangfujing? We'll meet at whichever mall you're most familiar with," suggested Li-An.

"None are familiar to me. I'm now on the highway to Beijing (G6). It's pretty congested, so not sure if I can arrive on time." White followed with a picture of the google map showing the G6 highway.

"I was at Zhangjiakou the past couple days. I didn't expect the road to be so congested today. Otherwise, I could have arrived Beijing earlier."

Zhangjiakou was a famous ski resort in Hebei province, next to Beijing city. The day before, White had posted a short video clip on LetsChat of him sliding down a gentle slope but accidentally slipping and falling as he landed on flatter ground. His ability to laugh at himself struck her as endearing.

"Tell me where you are and I'll find you," he added.

"Come straight to Jinbao street". It meant Golden Treasure Street. So many names of things in China related to wealth, or good luck in attaining it. "I'm staying at Park Plaza Hotel, 95 Golden Treasure Street."

"Got it. Stay in your room. Come down only when I arrive at the hotel lobby." Li-An didn't like the slightly commanding tone, though she realized he was trying to be polite. She responded with an ok hand sign.

2nd January 2017, 5.15 pm

A new message from White flashed onto Li-An's phone. She clicked on the LetsChat app to read it, but it turned out to be another google map. At the top was a string of Chinese characters, but Li-An only recognized Badaling, where she'd been a few years ago to see a section of the Great Wall. She reckoned he was showing her his current whereabouts.

"?" she wrote nevertheless.

"The road just cleared. I'll only reach your place 7-ish." He added a frowning emoticon after the message. "If you're hungry, go have something first. I'll treat you to whatever you want to eat later." His message was followed by a Kungfu salute – an outstretched left palm over and on a closed right fist.

2nd January 2017, 7.06 pm

"Where are you?" Li-An was getting impatient. It was past seven and he still hadn't arrived.

"On the subway. Seven more stops to go." Plus an emoticon with sweat to express his anxiety. Li-An was puzzled as to why he was now taking the subway, but figured the car he'd been in belonged to someone else, and they'd dropped him at a station.

"Take it slowly, then. Don't rush." At least now she knew he wasn't far away.

"Are you hungry?" he asked.

"No."

"I'm almost there. What a feat!" An emoticon with one hand cupping the mouth, apparently to stifle a laughter. "How expressive he is," she thought.

2nd January 2017, 7.25 pm

"I'm here at the lobby."

"Hao. Ok," Li-An replied.

When she got to the lobby, she found White sitting facing the direction of the lifts, but he was looking down at the table so didn't see her walking towards him. "Bai Xiang." Li-An called out. He immediately stood up but continued to direct his gaze downwards. Sensing his nervousness, Li-An decided to initiate. "Let's walk to that restaurant over there." She pointed to a place with a green signboard just across the road from the hotel. "Hao," replied White. As they walked side-by-side, Li-An noticed he was about an inch taller than her. A nice feeling. Her fiancé was shorter than Li-An, and never felt like a protective presence standing next to her. They were silent throughout the two-minute journey. But Li-An was quietly enjoying the experience of walking with him. He somehow made her feel safe.

It was a respectable little family restaurant serving Cantonese fare. As they took off their winter jackets, Li-An noticed White was wearing a top that matched the design on her dress. The black stripes. The only difference was that the design on his top was slanted instead of vertical.

"We have matching outfits," Li-An commented as she sat down.

White seemed embarrassed and didn't reply, straightaway flipping open the menu.

"What do you like to eat?" he asked.

"I'm actually not that hungry," Li-An replied, "but I don't mind something light, like vegetables."

"How about a soup dish?" He pointed to a picture on the menu. Li-An saw slivers of pork.

"And zhushi?" Main dish. Obviously, Li-An's comment about not being hungry hadn't registered with him.

"And how about this clay pot rice with roast pork?" asked White.

Li-An hesitated to say yes. Hadn't she said vegetables? But she knew it was Chinese custom to order a lot of expensive food in the presence of guests. Their way of showing hospitality. She gave in and agreed to the order, thinking he'd eat most of it.

"Fuwuyuan!" he shouted to the lone waitress in the restaurant. As he ordered the food, Li-An made a quick scan of the restaurant. They were the only customers that night because of the New Year holiday.

After taking the order, the waitress left for the kitchen. He turned and looked down at the table for a moment, as though preparing something in his mind, and then quickly raised his head.

"What do you look for in a man?" he said. Seemingly embarrassed by his own question, he quickly shifted his gaze to one corner of the room while he waited for her answer.

"I don't know." Li-An was taken aback by his directness. Where was the small talk?

Not knowing what to say next, White looked down again, but this time at his shoes. Just then, a message flashed on the phone which he'd placed on the table to his left. He picked it up, swiped the surface with a flick of his right index finger, and quickly keyed in a few characters. Li-An was certain it was a message from his girlfriend asking if he'd safely arrived in Beijing. As he put the phone back down on the table, she decided to switch to a lighter topic.

"How old are you?" she asked.

"Twenty-nine," he answered. He didn't ask for Li-An's age, assuming he was older than her. After all, Li-An had nodded her head in the plane that morning when he asked if she was in her twenties. But she'd also assumed he was older than he turned out to be. Only now did she realize he was a full decade younger than her!

"Oh, I see," replied Li-An as she shifted her gaze to the right.

Again, White looked down and started fiddling with his watch. Li-An noticed that it looked expensive.

"So you like skiing?" she asked, determined to move away from their previous conversation.

White nodded his head and went on to explain that he was based in Hebei province, where there was skiing, as well as Beijing. He also confirmed that the company he worked for was among the top real estate developers in China. The CEO was a southerner who'd started in the 80s when China was just opening up. He eventually made it big, cultivating the right connections, and extended his business all over the country, and now even internationally.

"So your clientele are mainly rich people?" asked Li-An.

"Yes, but they're mostly those who'd owned lands and properties which our government bought over. With huge payouts." Just as White was explaining to Li-An, the waitress arrived with the food.

"I see. So, the property market is good right now?" she asked.

"Yes, at least that's what it'll be like for the next couple years. Come let's eat." The waitress had scooped two bowlfuls of soup and placed one of them on Li-An's side of the table. As they ate, Li-An was thinking to herself about the *New York Times* article she'd read just before coming to China, where western papers were mostly unavailable. According to that source the Chinese economy was stagnant, and real estate in particular. Was he just talking big to impress her? But she decided not to challenge him.

"It's good, isn't it? Hen yangsheng (It's very nourishing)," he said, commenting on the soup served in a deep clay pot dish. Li-An nodded smilingly.

"So, does your company provide housing or do you have to rent at your own expense?"

"My company provides accommodation. The female colleagues live in separate dorm from the guys."

"That's the same situation as my friends at the university" she said.

Li-An had learned from her time in China that the country operated on a dual economy. While China had clearly adopted a form of capitalism, official institutions like universities still retained socialist vestiges from the Mao era. One was a lifetime pension. Li-An was told by her friend – her fiancé's secretary – that the monthly payout of her pension would be more than the salary that she was currently drawing. Even though the secretary was in her mid-30s, she and many of Li-An's friends working in the Chinese university system were already looking forward to retirement. Another was the free housing system. Li-An's fiancé made it just in time for the last "house distribution" – fenfang – exercise before Chinese leaders decided it was too much of a toll on the national coffers, and ended it. "She wanted a free apartment, and that's why we got married," Grey had admitted one day as to why he'd married his former wife.

"Da bu liao bu gan!" "I can always quit if I don't like it!" blurted out White. His tone was almost strained. He must have thought Li-An's question about company housing was to sound out his eligibility as a partner, and his answer had revealed a black mark: his lack of property. But she'd just been trying to make conversation.

Now it was Li-An who didn't know what to say, knowing she'd touched on a sensitive topic. She quietly lowered her head and focused on eating her dinner. She couldn't square White's expressive messages on LetsChat – all the emoticons - with his reticence and nervousness in person.

A few moments later, she raised her head slightly to find White looking at her intently. She smiled. He smiled back.

"That development project belonging to your company. Forest something." Li-An turned her head slightly to the left and frowned as she tried to recall its name.

"Paradise," White quickly added.

"Yes, Forest Paradise"

"Why? Are you interested?"

"I just want to find out more. Given that property prices are so high in Kramen, I'm exploring the option of investing in cheaper housing off-shore. Maybe even Forest Paradise." Again, she was trying to talk about things he knew.

"Hmmm..." He nodded his head but his facial expression was one of surprised doubt.

"I've probably got the cash to make the down payment for a one-bedroom apartment." But Li-An quickly stopped herself, thinking she'd given too much away about her financial status.

White broke into spontaneous laughter, smothering it a few seconds later. Needless to say, Li-An felt insulted. Did he think that a girl as young as she appeared to be couldn't possibly afford a Forest Paradise apartment? In any case he wasn't taking her seriously.

"If you're that keen, just call the office and give them my employee number." Or was he insulted too? Did he think she'd accepted his invitation because of business rather than pleasure?

"So, you're leaving Beijing tomorrow?" he asked. Li An nodded in response. By now, she was irritated, bored, and eager to end the dinner.

"By the way, I need to leave in about 20 minutes. I have some business to attend to," she said. Less than thirty minutes had passed since they stepped into the restaurant, and the food was half-eaten.

"Ok. You should have stayed in Beijing a little longer," he said.

"No, I'm here on transit. My destination is Harbin," replied Li-An.

"I could've brought you sightseeing."

"Actually, I came to Beijing to buy myself a qipao. That's why I'm staying at this hotel. I saw a couple specialty shops a few years back. But now they're gone. I guess hulianwang (e-commerce) has really taken over," she said regretfully.

"Yes, now you can buy anything from the internet," White remarked agreeably.

"And you certainly look very nice in a qipao." With both his hands, White drew an outline of an ideal woman's figure in the air. She was startled, not so much by his boldness as the fact that he couldn't actually see her figure in the dress she was wearing. Then it struck her. Her LetsChat site included a listing of past postings, in chronological order. Had he come across that picture of her in a silky peach-pink cheongsam? Its white prints were recognizably Chinese, but not so tacky that Li-An looked like a waitress. The halter neck-collar showed off her broad shoulders, and the fit of the dress complimented her curves. Her hair was in a pony-tail, and gelled, giving her whole look an attractive glow. Li-An had worn it for an evening function. He'd had to have scrolled deeply into her feed to find that photo, because it was posted in July last year, and it was now January.

"You are a woman with many fine qualities. What type of man do you look for?" White repeated his first question to Li-An, with more confidence but no less inappropriateness.

"I don't know," she said again, following it with an even more cultivated silence.

"Don't you already have a girlfriend?" she asked.

"She's not quite suitable." White turned his eyes away as she seized the upper ground.

"Look, I do have to go now." Li-An put her chopsticks down.

Li-An waited for him to pay the bill, then stood up to put on her winter scarf and jacket. She saw from the corner of her eye that he was stealing quick glances at her body. Quietly, they walked back to the hotel. Just as they reached the lift, she stopped and turned to face him.

"Thank you for dinner." She held out her right hand.

"Come and visit Beijing more often" said White as he reached out to shake it.

Li-An smiled, then quickly turned to press the lift button. The door opened instantly and she entered without bothering to turn and check if he was still staring after her.

"Twenty-nine years old. Certainly didn't look it on the plane." Li-An let out a long sigh as the lift made its way up to her floor. "But he did act it."

Back in her room, Li-An started getting ready for bed. She'd showered earlier that evening, so took just a few minutes to brush her teeth and change into her pajamas. Once she'd gotten comfortable under the down feather quilt, she reached for the cylindrical pill box labeled "Xter" on the side table to her right. Up until now, Li-An had been discreet enough not to set the pill box outside her purse, even when alone, and as ordinary as it looked. During her hosteling days, she'd made sure to always keep the pills in the personal locker assigned to her. And if she was sharing the hotel room with Grey, Li-An would hide the box in the day and at night secretly sneak a pill into the bathroom, popping it only after she'd finished preparing herself for bed. Or sex. The pill took exactly fifteen minutes and thirty seconds to knock her out.

2nd January 2017, 9.20 pm

"I've just gotten into the subway," reported White. "Sleep early tonight."

"Goodnight." Li-An added an emoticon with a rosy-cheeked face, the edges of the lip almost touching both eyes. She thought it looked cute.

"Ok. Looking forward to our next meet up," he replied. "By the way, why are you frowning?" He was referring to Li-An's choice of the emoticon.

"What do you mean?" she asked.

"That expression that you just sent out. It's a frowning one," explained White.

"Is that so? I just thought it looked cute. That's all." By now, Li-An could barely open her eyes. The pill had taken its effect.

"I see. Goodnight."

Li-An didn't respond but turned off her phone and immediately closed her eyes to sleep. The next evening, she knew, she'd be leaving for Harbin on the overnight train.

5 HARBIN INTERLUDE

. The train ride to Harbin was calming, but also filled with mystery and anticipation. A Kramean like Li-An, living in a country with no trains, could not take an overnight sleeper without feeling herself in a scene from an old movie. She wanted privacy, so had paid for two soft berths. The compartment had a table by the window, and there was a bench she could use for her suitcase. The toilet near the entrance came with two toothbrush sets – their boxes had a picture of a train in bright Mao-era colors: reds, oranges, and greens. Li-An counted. It was only seven foot-lengths from one end of the compartment to the other. But she felt safe and cozy. Except for the sound of the train chugging on towards Harbin and the regular click-click rhythm of the wheels on the track, there was absolute silence. The excited giggles of the child next door had long since died down.

Looking out the window she saw her own reflection amid the falling snow. She flashed back to the scene nineteen years before, when her boyfriend had fondled her on her first-ever flight, and she'd watched her tears in the plane window. But now she was alone and safe in the confinement of a train cabin. She turned and laid flat on the bed, closed her eyes, and soon gave in to the effects of the Xter pill. Nobody would touch her or hurt her on this trip.

The train arrived at Harbin early next morning, and Li-An joined the long taxi queue. When it was finally her turn, she told the driver to bring her to the Kempinski Hotel. Her third five-star hotel after Tianjin and Beijing. She was determined to pamper herself. The world-famous Harbin Ice Festival would open that night, and there were so many other places to explore during the day, according to her internet research. Harbin didn't look like anyplace else in China given the strong influence of Russian architecture. Passing the onion-domed Sophia church on the way to the hotel, Li-An felt as though she'd indeed crossed the border into Siberia.

Li-An felt free.

Free from Kramen Island, where Professor Evans and his team had been pressuring her for their 'deliverable'.

Free from her fiancé, whom she realized she could never truly love. But what exactly is love, she wondered? Li-An couldn't recall a moment when she'd actually felt it. All the men she'd slept with were merely 'human subjects', like her. Sex was just a physical act to bring momentary pleasure. Or violence, when perverse ones crossed her path. There was almost a pattern in the men Li-An attracted. Still, she'd made sure never to invest her emotions. But how could that continue, she asked herself. She knew that a part of her craved intimacy.

The ice festival was worth the trip. Castles, palaces, and every other kind of fantasy architecture extended to the horizon, all made from blocks of ice, and lit with dozens of bright colors by hidden lights. Lovers strolled on crenelated parapets, and families bunched in tight for pictures in front of ice gates and drawbridges. Children cut loose from their parents and ran up and down ice towers, around ice battlements, through ice tunnels. Their laughter becoming wisps of vapor in the frozen air. Li-An was taken back to her own childhood. Hadn't she been equally happy, running around Kramen playgrounds with their sandboxes, swings, and big dragon-slides? Why did the bad memories come so easily but the good ones require so much effort?

On the second day, Li-An visited the Siberian Tiger Park. The tigers roamed around the park freely, big and obviously well-fed. None of them were "Siberian", that is white with black stripes, except for one solitary tiger who was kept alone in a cage. The rest were the orange and black variety, likely imported from India, or artificially bred. The tourists, who observed them from snaking raised walkways, had the option of buying live chickens, pheasants, or even goats to feed to the cats. The park not only housed tigers. There were other big cats - a puma, a jaguar, and a black panther. None of them belonged in China, she thought, especially this cold province. Unlike the tigers, who roamed free, these more exotic cats were kept in small concrete enclosures, near the caged Siberian tiger. For a long time, Li-An stood and watched the jaguar and panther, in their separate cells, pace around and around in circles. Their heads remained drooped as they walked about aimlessly. She could see the defeat in their eyes.

Back in her hotel room that night, Li-An spent hours in the bathtub, her eyes staring blankly into space, and thinking about the lifeless souls of those animals. When she eventually got out of the bath and wiped herself clean, she reached for her mobile phone lying next to the basin. She went into LetsChat, searched for White's message board, and sent the best photo she'd taken of the ice festival.

5th January 2017, 8.15 pm

"It's beautiful," he replied within seconds

6 XTER TRIALS

Year: 2001   Location: Sentacruz, Kramen Island

Day 1 50 mg of Xter   Time of administration: 3 pm
Li-An felt drowsy, and just closed her eyes to sleep.

Day 2 8 am
Li-An woke up extremely agitated. She felt there were things inside her head, alive and crawling, like ants. Someone knocked on her door. It was Samantha. There was another woman with her. Her assistant. "How are you feeling right now?" Samantha asked. "There's something in my head. I don't know what it is, but I'm very uncomfortable." Li-An cowered as she spoke, her arms over her head. "It's the dosage, we need to cut it." Samantha gave an eye signal to her assistant, who coaxed Li-An back to bed and laid a blanket over her. "Take this. It should relieve some of the symptoms." Samantha extended her right arm, with a small blue pill in her outstretched palm. Li-An grabbed and swallowed it without question. It didn't take long for the drug to knock her out, and she fell back into a deep sleep.

Li-An dreamt. It was a scene from her childhood. She was seven. Her father was driving the family home. They were about to reach their apartment when her father pulled over in front of the neighborhood's mom-and-pop store to pick up an order. The rest of the family waited in the car. Li-An was singing with her sisters at the back when her mother, who was sitting in the passenger seat, broke her silence. "If he was still alive today, you girls would never have a place in this family." Li-An's mother didn't turn to look at her daughters but remained staring straight ahead, as if the remark was meant for no one but herself. Li-An heard it nevertheless. "Ma, who are you talking about?" asked Li-An. "Your brother, your dead brother" continued her mother. "You know, when you girls were still in my tummy, your father never brought me for my regular check-ups. But it was so different with your brother. And the few days that he was alive, your father stayed up late to take care of him. Never with you girls. He barely set his eyes on you when you were born." "But how did he die?" asked Li-An innocently. "High fever. And it's your fault. Your father was so upset he even thought of sending you away." Just then, Li-An's father emerged from the store. "Hush!" instructed her mom. Her father got into the car, switched on the engine and drove the family home. Throughout the journey, Li-An rested her forehead on the back of the passenger seat and teared quietly. For her dead brother. And for the idea that, somehow, it was her fault.

Day 3 10 am

Li-An felt dazed. It was both the work of the pills and the dream. She had her breakfast as usual, but instead of heading straight for her room, decided to go sit in the lobby. She wanted to restore the calm she'd felt when she'd first arrived at the hotel. But instead of feeling peaceful as she sat among the frangipani trees, Li-An began to recollect other scenes from her childhood, as though the dream had opened a secret door she couldn't close. Vague scenes she'd never remembered until now. The living room. Li-An and her sister were both on the floor playing at cooking. Their parents sat on the couch, and Li-An saw her mom sobbing incessantly. She stood up, her hand holding a toy cup, and slowly walked towards her mom. "Ma, don't cry. I've made some soup. Drink some and you'll get well soon," consoled Li-An. She was stirring the cup with a toy plastic spoon as she spoke, pretending there was actual soup. Li-An's mom didn't respond. "Go, go and play with your sister," her father commanded. Li-An turned and walked away obediently. Because of the dream she'd had the day before, she knew her mother was crying over the death of her newborn son.

She closed her eyes and the scene shifted, earlier in time. It was the usual weekend gathering at her paternal grandparents' place. Li-An's mom was still pregnant with her brother. Her tummy was showing it. Night fell. It was time to head home. Li-An, her mother, and her sister took the lift to the ground floor, where Li-An's father was waiting at the nearby open-air carpark. The lift door opened, and her sister quickly dashed for their father's car, which was separated from the lift by a slope and a ditch. The slope was a gentle one and the ditch not too wide for a five-year-old to jump over. Li-An's mother too had opted for the slope, a much shorter route than the roundabout walkway. But it'd rained earlier that day and the ground was slippery. Li-An was holding her hand when her mother began to fall into the ditch. She released Li-An's hand in time, so her daughter was safe. But the ditch was narrow and deep. She got up but had scratches and bruises all over her. She was worried about the baby.

It might have been fine if her mother had applied only cream or ointment, since it was an external injury. Li-An wanted to say so in the dream, but she was just a little girl, and powerless. She saw her mother taking oral medication. A prescription from a Western doctor and some Chinese drug her aunt recommended. It could have been a case of contraindication. No one would ever know. She saw her mother bring Li-An's baby brother home. She saw him die of severe jaundice three days later. His skin turned all yellow. Or maybe something else had caused that? She'd heard different explanations through the years. The dream didn't make it clearer.

Her eyes still closed, the scene shifted again. Li-An's parents were consulting a medium at a Daoist temple. They were grieving and looking for answers. The woman said they were not destined to have a son. "Either mother or son go. Or both go." Li-An's mother then recalled an incident and interpreted it as an omen. "Yes, I remember," she said to the medium, "I was walking along the road one day. I was still carrying him in my tummy then. It was raining very heavily and suddenly a tree fell right in front of me. If I'd made a step further, I'd have been crushed by it. Both of us would have been killed. Me and my unborn son."

Now Li-An was remembering with eyes open. She was overhearing her parents' conversation one evening, as they traced the root cause of their son's death to the night when Li-An's mom fell into the ditch. Instead of blaming himself for parking the car too far away, her father decided it was Li-An who'd caused the death of his son. Because his wife was holding his daughter's hand. Taking too much care of the little girl. It had interfered with her balance.

After that leap of logic, Li-An's position in the family would never be the same.

Day 4 8 am

Li-An noticed something was wrong as soon as she opened her eyes. She looked around her, but she could only see straight ahead. She'd lost her peripheral vision, like a horse with blinders. She was worried for sure, but the welling sense of panic was somehow subdued by another symptom. A coating. There was a thick coating extending over her brain. Like a protective layer.

"Yes, it's the pill alright. It's taking effect." replied Samantha, who didn't look particularly concerned.

"We cut it to 25 mg," Samantha ran her finger over Li-An's med record. "Not a lot, but you're one of the sensitive ones. Don't worry though, everyone goes through some version of what you're experiencing." Her eyes were still glued to Li-An's dossier.

"What do you mean?" Li-An looked up, but not at Samantha, who was standing to her right, and thus out of her line of vision.

"Xter's designed to transform you completely. And that includes your brain chemistry. There's no getting around it. In most cases it gets rid of your demons. Your emotional baggage. So you need to suffer through some bad memories for the magic to happen. In your dreams and even when you're not dreaming." Samantha spoke with a superior air, enhanced by her horn-rimmed glasses. Li-An doubted Samantha ever had any demons of her own.

"What magic?" Li-An was not looking at Samantha but straight ahead as though she was blind.

"Your cells. Actually, your chromosomes. They're going to be transformed. And eventually your looks. But there's a lot that happens in your mind first. Be patient." Samantha, now standing in front of Li-An, pointed her right index finger and slightly puckered her lips as she spoke the last two words. They were more an order than an encouraging suggestion.

"But, don't worry. You're in good hands." Samantha's tone suddenly softened and she gently placed her hands on Li-An's shoulder. "Just imagine how beautiful you'll look when this is finished. Remember, the keyword is patience." Samantha winked at Li-An, followed by a smile. Then she quickly turned and walked away, not waiting for a reaction. Li-An's gaze followed Samantha until she turned a corner and disappeared.

This place, thought Li-An, this Lab of Possibilities, was mainly about the possibilities of science. Not her own. It was devoid of feelings and emotions, except for the hurtful ones it was creating inside her brain. Samantha's hand on her shoulder – and her smile – had given Li-An the first small feeling of warmth and comfort she'd had since arriving, however fleeting and insincere. But she had to trust them now. It had started.

Day 5 1 pm.
Li-An was sunbathing by the pool under the sweltering heat. She'd made an effort to walk normally and not show her lack of peripheral vision. She sat reclining on the wooden deck chair, tilted sharply at a 45-degree angle. There was a thick cushion and she had a cool drink by her side, so didn't feel terribly uncomfortable. Only that the people walking back and forth around the swimming pool were no longer humans. They were animals. Giraffes, rhinos, elephants, etc. Big game. There was still that coating over her head, and it kept Li-An from feeling threatened to be among so much wildlife. It felt like an invisible protective barrier between her and the animals. As though they couldn't see her. She felt she was using synapses that had never been fully activated. The pill was suddenly pushing deep but vague memories to the surface and into the light. The only problem was that her memories came in unchronological snippets. And they were almost never good ones.

Even with her eyes open the images would start to play, like a movie. It was the year 1997. Li-An was in her second year of Anglo-Asia Junior College. Or AAJC for short. Arts stream. Literature, History, Mathematics, Economics, and General Paper. While she'd had no problem with mathematics, Li-An struggled with the rest of the subjects, having been brought up in a Chinese-speaking household with limited exposure to English, even in school. But Li-An liked a good challenge and so chose a stream that she thought she'd eventually conquer with constant practice, as she had math. She just hadn't anticipated the stigma her Chinese language background would carry. Language policed class relations in Kramen. Ethnically Chinese students of AAJC were proud to show, or even pretend, that they sucked at Chinese. Li-An loved the language, in which she was fluent. But she sucked at English, her country's official and higher-status language, so was despised by her peers and teachers.

The pills focused her mind on one moment in particular. "Who is Zhu Li-An?" asked her lit teacher one afternoon during class. Li-An immediately raised her hand, thinking she was about to be praised for their very first assignment. "Who taught you English?! And which lousy school did you come from?!! Your grammar is atrocious! You think in Chinese when writing in English. The world belongs to those who can speak and write good English. Get it!" Li-An fought hard not to cry by opening her eyes so wide they almost filled her glasses.

It might not have been so bad for her if her father was wealthy. AAJC was largely for the Kramen elite. Before she was accepted there, Li-An had only gone to "neighborhood schools", a derogatory term for public schools attended by regular Krameans. Li-An thought she could shake off her lower middle-class roots by enrolling in a prestigious junior college. Wearing the AAJC uniform could mask her real identity. While Li-An's grades were good enough to enter any of Kramen Island's top five junior colleges, she'd stubbornly put her mind on getting into AAJC, because it seemed cooler than the rest. She had yet to make the connection between cool and rich. But it hit her forcefully on the first week of school. Big luxury cars – Mercedes Benz, Rolls Royce, Audis – lined up at the entrance each morning and late afternoon, as parents or even real chauffeurs dropped her classmates at school.

As for Li-An, she'd arrive at school in her father's cab. She was naïve at first. When her classmates saw her get out of a cab one morning, they mistook her for someone rich enough to afford daily taxi-fare. One girl, who turned out to be the wealthiest in the class, lamented how her own father found her too spendthrift and decided to discipline her by making her find her own way to school every day. Li-An, not wanting to put on airs, said "Oh, no, that's my father. He drives a cab." "Oh really," sneeringly replied another of Li-An's classmates, and the group started looking at one another, quickly turned their backs on her and walked away.

Taxi-driver was a new identity for Li-An's father, which the family were all still grappling with. He'd owned a small ship-building company, but shut it down and instead turned to stock investing. Being impulsive, Li-An's father lost big time. By then, Li-An's father was already in his late forties so could not find employment in his field. Cab driving was his only option. He sold his Mercedes Benz but was too ashamed to be seen with his taxi, so would park it at a far distance from the family's apartment building. His only consolation was that he still had rent from some properties he'd bought when he was flush.

After the incident with the girls, Li-An was embarrassed to have her father take her to school. She began sitting at the back of her father's cab so that she looked more like a passenger. And when she saw a classmate swish by in a luxury car, she'd instinctively push her body back so as not to be seen. Sensing Li-An's behavior, her father too began acting out his insecurity. He'd drop her off at the main road instead of turning into the school's entrance. One morning, the radio broadcast an interview with a student who'd emerged as the top scholar in the college entrance examinations. When asked what his father did, the student replied "he's a taxi driver". Li-An's father immediately turned up the volume so that Li-An could hear the interview. She did not reward him with a comment.

At least they all wore the same school uniforms. The girls. But when they took them off in the locker-room for gym class or swimming, it all changed. Li-An was shocked to see how comfortable the other girls were stripping naked in front of each other. Back in the neighborhood schools where she'd come from, girls were so shy about showing off their bodies. Li-An was embarrassed about hers even though, objectively speaking, she could compete with the best of them. But worse was when they put on their swim-suits, because they weren't issued by the school. The costumes were the fanciest Li-An had ever seen. Expensive-looking and fashionably designed. Li-An's memory was drawn to the cutest girl of their cohort, who wore a neon orange one piece topped with frilly straps. Li-An had only a dull-looking two-piece suit, nearly the opposite of that svelte colorful suit of – what was her name? Her Christian name was Samantha. Tan. Samantha Tan!

Li-An's head jolted forward as she suddenly regained her present self. Could this Samantha Tan be her former classmate? Or

Clarissa? Which one? Which was the real person, and which the clone? Li-An was distracted by a movement in the far distance. A roaming peacock. But as it came closer, Li-An realized it was an actual human. And it turned out to be one of the clone sisters.

"Clarissa?" Whichever one she was had stopped at Li-An's feet.

"No, Samantha," she replied.

"Did you go to AAJC?" The bright sun made Li-An squint her eyes.

"Yes. Batch 1996-1997. AD 3. I remember you too." Li-An caught a note of snideness in Samantha's voice, but she was more shocked than insulted. To realize that the prettiest girl from their junior college became a test subject like herself!

"But why are you here? You were already so beautiful. What happened?" Li-An couldn't contain her curiosity.

Samantha didn't answer. She just smiled surreptitiously, turned, and went on her way. It was a set of gestures Li-An knew well. As she walked toward the lobby of the hotel, Samantha turned back into a peacock in Li-An's mind and vision, her plumage spread in a colorful semi-circle.

One week later 6.30 am

It was dawn. Li-An woke up earlier than usual. Like on most mornings now, she vividly remembered the dream she'd had the night before. She knew they weren't dreams in the sense of being unreal, the products of subconscious imaginings. They were painfully accurate flashbacks. Re-opened chambers of memory she'd kept tightly locked. She'd come here to escape from her family. But the therapy vividly thrust them back into her consciousness. And as pieces of a puzzle she was being made to assemble against her will. This had never been in the contract.

Li-An was twelve. She was taking a nap in her own bedroom in their two-story maisonette. With her father reduced to driving a cab on full shift seven days a week, Li-An's mom naturally felt lonely. She had only married to escape poverty, and had no real goals in life to fill the emptiness. So she'd begun to do weird things, like undressing herself on the balcony. Their maisonette was only four stories high with eight households. Opposite was a tall block of flats, and anyone living from the fifth story upwards could easily look into Li-An's house. Her mom frequently told her children to watch out for peeping toms, and they kept their windows mostly shuttered, leaving only a small gap for ventilation. Which made it all the stranger for Li-An that her mother would undress on the open balcony, even removing her bra.

The dream opened with Li-An taking a nap, and vaguely hearing a stranger talking. It was a man's voice. "I always see you in the balcony. I live opposite you." "Go! Go away!" Now it was Li-An's mother's voice. The young Li-An forced herself to wake up, but by the time she went down to the first story of their house, the commotion had stopped. The man had gone. "What happened?" asked Li-An half awake. "Nothing. Go back up to your room," replied her mom. "Tell me what happened?" Li-An turned to look at her elder sister who'd witnessed the whole incident, but Li-An's mom gave a look that signaled her to clam up. "Nothing happened! Just go back to your room and study!" She did. But later, when she saw her mother sitting in the kitchen looking scared and disturbed, she was emboldened to approach her again. "What happened, Ma?" she asked gently "who was that man just now? Did he really see into our balcony from up there?" she asked. "His mouth was full of blood. I gave him fifty dollars and told him never to come here again," said her mother. It would never be clear to Li-An why the man was bleeding in the mouth.

Li-An's dream reeled back further in time, before they'd upgraded to the maisonette, when they still lived in a small apartment on the thirteenth story of an old public housing building. Thirteen. An unlucky number. Li-An used to associate her string of unfortunate childhood events to the floor she first lived on. One event had to do with her mother's habit of not wearing a bra at home. Whenever she returned from shopping at the market, or anywhere, she would immediately remove it in a clever way. First, she'd unhook the buckle from underneath her blouse. Then, she'd bring her upper arms– one following the other – back into her shirt through the sleeves and remove the straps from her shoulders. Finally, a pull and presto! the bra came sliding out of one sleeve in a quick motion. Li-An and her elder sister would giggle whenever her mom performed the act for them. It was like a magic trick. But then again, Li-An's mom was never consistent about putting the bra back on when strangers or neighbors knocked on their door, which Li-An found disturbing. "Ma, why didn't you wear your bra? Do you know that he could see through your shirt?"

In the dream, Li-An's mom was watering the potted plants lining on the corridor outside their house, and as usual was bra-less. The shirt she was wearing happened to have a broad collar such that whenever she bent over to lift up the plants, her breasts were exposed. It so happened that their neighbor's husband had taken time off from work that day and was resting at home. He'd deliberately sat on the steps in front of Li-An's apartment in order to see her mother's breasts. There were children around. Li-An and her sister, and the neighbor's own children, so Li-An decided to do something. She stood in front of her mother and followed her wherever she went, masking her breasts with her own small body. Li-An would ask questions about the plants she was watering, like what were their names and how should each one be cared for. Despite her efforts, Li-An knew deep down that her neighbor had caught glimpses of her mother's breasts. Once inside, she confronted her mother. "Well, who cares whether he sees me? All the better for him," was her reply.

One week and a half later 6 am

For the past week and a half, Li-An had consistently woken at dawn. Six-ish. And covered in sweat. This morning she decided to head straight for the shower. As the water drizzled heavily down on her hair, she succumbed to its weight and drooped her head down. She looked intently, yet at the same time dreamily, at the turquoise-colored floor tiles which turned blurry as the water cascaded over them. Her mind drifted back to the dream she'd had the night before.

Li-An was very young, aged six or seven. She'd grown to like the scent of her own vagina. When no one was watching – for some reason she knew it was taboo even at that age – Li-An would slip her fingers into her panties, wet them with the scent of her vagina and then smell them. In her dream Li-An was lying flat on the marbled flooring of their apartment, her legs raised and propped up on a chair. She felt the urge to reach inside her panties. Just as she did, her mom entered the living room and caught her in the act. Fuming, she beat her with the short cane that almost every Kramen household used to have to beat children with. Not satisfied with the beating, she also burned Li-An on both her thighs with the end of a burning incense stick.

For weeks, the cane and burn marks served as reminders to Li-An not to touch herself again. They also served to shame Li-An in front of others, for her mother had hit her in places she couldn't cover in her clothes. "Did your mom hit you again?" asked Li-An's classmate who was sitting next to her in the classroom. Their school uniform had short sleeves, so Li-An couldn't hide that long cane mark on her right arm. She responded to her classmate with silence. It was punishment for a shameful act, so she couldn't possibly explain. But no need really. Her mom would beat her daughters – but especially Li-An – so often that it was no longer a novelty to Li-An's friends. Thank god, however, that they couldn't see the burn marks on her thighs.

Now the dream was at her grandmother's house, where they used to visit on Saturdays. She was on the floor drawing pictures when she heard her mother in the next room going on about the episode and how she'd burnt Li-An on the thighs. Half-smiling and half-concerned, Li-An's granny came into the room and lifted her skirt to see the three burn marks, two on her right thigh and one on her left. "It's very shameful, you know. Don't do it again," said Li-An's granny, stifling laughter while Li-An fought back tears by biting hard at the back of her lips. As her granny left the room, Li-An crossed the paper she was drawing on as hard as she could with the colored pencil, leaving a long tear.

One hundred days later

By the hundredth day, Li-An was overwhelmed. Ever since taking her first Xter pill, she was experiencing constant changes in her body and mind. The coating over her head persisted. While the pill forced her to recall traumatic episodes from her past, it also dulled her mind in the present. So much so that Li-An couldn't even bring herself to read a short magazine article, not to mention a book. Now Li-An knew why Samantha had given her a curious stare when she asked on the first day if there was a library at the hotel. Most of the time she'd sit on her balcony starring aimlessly at the sky or the grounds, or following the pairs of peacocks (real ones) strutting around the resort. Her vision also continued to be affected. Humans no longer appeared to her as animals. But her eyeballs did not move, even when she talked to someone. They stared straight ahead. Staff of the hotel were now familiar with the effects wrought by the Xter pill so didn't treat Li-An any differently from when she first arrived. But guests at the resort would occasionally mistake Li-An for a blind person and give up their seat to her in the lounge or by the pool.

The flashbacks left Li-An wondering at how much shit she'd allowed herself to be put through all these years. Rejection from her parents ever since her brother's death; her mother's daring showcasing of her body; sibling rivalry, et cetera, et cetera. Her ex-boyfriend, or rather that perverted asshole, was just one of a long list of characters whom she'd had to suffer. A couple knocks on the door startled Li-An, who instantly dropped the fruit knife she was holding near to her right wrist.

"There you are. We were looking for you." Li-An opened the door and saw Samantha with her arms crossed and frowning.

"You have an appointment with Professor Evans. You were supposed to meet me at the lab. Have you forgotten?"

"I... I'm sorry... I was just..." As always, Samantha didn't wait for Li-An to finish her sentence but turned to walk away. Li-An quickly followed behind her.

"I know what this is all about now," said Li-An to Evans as he approached her. There was that same spotlight following him, except that it was now aiming even lower: at his feet. She could see that the professor's face had deteriorated even further since their first meeting. Flakier with more creases, and worsened by his attempt to hide them using even thicker foundation. But Li-An didn't pay much attention to Evans' appearance. "I want out, I can't take it anymore. Either kill me or let me go." Li-An's voice was breaking.

The professor was unfazed, as though her outburst was utterly normal. He walked past Li-An and went to look through one of the microscopes. Li-An's eyes followed him. "Did you listen, I said I want out!" she said with a raised voice. "Calm down and let me explain what's happening to you," said Evans. "You're going through what I call reverse engineering. You remember what the name of the project is?" Li-An replied, "Project X". "But you missed the most important word, which is 'inverted'. Tell me, how does a chromosome look? "Like an x," she said. "And when you invert it what do you get?" "An x again". "Exactly!" he shouted. "Your chromosomes are in the process of inversion. As your body reverses its aging, your mind is reversing memory, and making you vividly relive thoughts you didn't know you had, but that never disappeared. Think of it as your mind going through a cleansing. I've looked at your chart, and you have the strongest reaction to Xter we've seen so far. But it just means you've come to us with more than the usual trauma."

"Yes, look at me," said Li-An, "I'm worse than when I first came here. This isn't what was promised." "Patience, patience," said Evans, "didn't my girls tell you to be patient? It's still working for you, despite the discomfort." "Yes they keep saying that," replied Li-An, "but give me a timeline. Two years is too long. This is only the hundredth day! This coating – I feel so trapped inside it. It'll never wear off, will it?" Li-An was now highly agitated. "As the saying goes, good things come to those who wait," he said dismissively. She hated him at that moment, but knew she wouldn't stop the treatment.

"Why did you come here? Did you take the pills too? Why did you let yourself be cloned!?" Li-An blurted out, as she followed Samantha back to her room.

"I know your family's rich. You were already beautiful. So why?" Samantha stopped and turned back to look at Li-An.

"Yes I took the pills. This project isn't just the government, you know. So you know who my parents are. Our pharmaceutical company, They're big investors. They got around the trust issue, the dodgy clinical trials, by investing their own flesh and blood," retorted Samantha, who looked at Li-An with such piercing anger that for a moment all her side effects seemed to disappear as she became fully focused.

"But... but... you could have said no," Li-An stuttered in fright.

"Well," said Samantha, "Let's put it this way, not everyone had a bad past like yours. I certainly didn't. Mine was easy. The rejuvenating effects of the drug kicked in by the 50th day."

She then leaned close and almost whispered into Li-An's ear.

"There's actually a way to trick the pill, or fight it, so that you don't need two years of this."

Li-An looked up, but not at Samantha. "How?"

"Remember happy incidents. You must have had some. Whenever bad memories creep in, don't let them overtake you. Quickly recall some happy moment. The pill will start to think that its cleansing work is done."

"But I hardly have any good memories," said Li-An.

"Try. Try very hard," said Samantha.

The Hundred and First Day

Things in the 13th floor apartment. A metal cabinet full of WWF and pornography tapes. WWF. The World Wrestling Federation. A pin-up poster of a blonde in sexy lingerie. They belonged to Li-An's father. Up till now Li-An only remembered her father as wanting to throw her out of the house after her brother died. This morning she started recalling him through his objects. Violent things. Sexual things. Things she should not have seen as a child. Those tapes. Every episode of WWF wrestling, which he played distractingly while Li-An tried to do homework. And even worse was the porn. She remembered waking up one morning as a little girl, after being told to shower and get ready for school, and seeing porn playing on the television. They'd temporarily shielded the TV screen with a cloth, thinking that was fine while Li-An prepared for classes, but she could still make out the scenes through the fabric.

"Stop!" Li-An thought. She remembered what Samantha told her the day before. Happy thoughts, good memories. She tried, but none immediately came to mind. Maybe she should just stop thinking. But no, the pill seemed to have taken over and one bad memory after another kept gushing into her head. "Try. Try harder." Slowly, she stood up, closed her eyes and began to breathe slowly and deeply.

Li-An's paternal grandfather. They were about to go out for a walk. Li-An was very young then, probably four or five years old. Her mom and grandmother were watching as Li-An's grandfather helped her tie her shoelaces. When they got down to the basement of the apartment building, they saw the ice-cream man. Li-An's grandfather bought her a popsicle. Li-An could not remember much about her grandfather's appearance to fill in the scene, or his voice, or manner, or anything else really. He'd suffered a stroke soon after their walk together and became paralyzed from the waist down. After that he'd stayed in his room and never went out of the house. Li-An would greet him whenever she visited, but never stayed by his side to chat. She was too young and didn't have the patience to listen to his soft murmurs. But it was still a good memory, about the popsicle. That was a start, Li-An consoled herself.

Then there was the memory of her paternal grandmother holding her grandchildren – Li-An's younger cousins – and coaxing them to poo over the newspaper spread out on the floor. "Mmm... mmm..." her grandmother would hum incessantly till she heard the dropping sound made by the poo. Li-An never failed to be amused by her cousins' naked asses. "Shame! Shame!" she'd tease even though they were too young to know what was happening. Just as Li-An thought she was beginning to defeat the pill, a painful memory forced its way into her head.

"You smelly pussy!", "You rotten smelly pussy!"

Li-An suddenly recalled her grandmother's stock phrase. Smelly pussy. She'd heard her grandmother scolding mother or aunts in that language. Li-An began to recall things her mother had said about life after marrying her father. "She knocked on my door very early the next day after the wedding dinner. I was just married but had to help her prepare breakfast for your uncles." Li-An's parents could not yet afford to buy an apartment and so lived with her grandparents and uncles. "Life with her was very hard. Work, work, and work." Li-An's mother described a typical day with her mother-in-law as nothing but cooking, cleaning, and cooking again. "I was like a maid to his family. Your father. He didn't show any concern and love to me. I remember one night, one of your uncles bought a big bag of durians. Your father didn't offer me any so I sat quietly at one corner while the rest of them ate." Li-An noticed her mom's eyes were welling up with tears. "But you could've helped yourself to some, no?" asked Li-An. "I didn't dare" was her mom's reply.

Her mother went on to describe how her mother-in-law, Li-An's grandmother, had despised her own family. Niang Jia. Literally "the maiden's home". Li-An's maternal grandmother was the mistress of an opium-smoker who'd squandered his wealth and ended up a noodle seller. Li-An remembered eating only once at her grandfather's stall. Wanton noodle. It was fairly well-known in the district where the stall was operated. Still, they could never get rich selling noodles. Li-An's father, on the other hand, had built a respectable shipbuilding business and managed to pull his family out of poverty and into relative prosperity. His business would later collapse, but until then he was considered the most successful among her grandmother's sons-in-law. Li-An's maternal grandmother had given birth to a long line of daughters and only one son, whereas her father's side was a family of six male siblings and only two sisters. When the two grandmothers met, Li-An noticed her maternal grandmother always addressed the other one with submissive deference.

"Stop! I have to stop thinking negative thoughts!" Li-An stood up from the balcony chair, and headed back into the room. She reached for the pen and stack of papers with the hotel letterhead – refilled every other day at housekeeping time – and began forcing herself to write down a list of happy childhood memories:

Sentacruz Resort and Spa
Kramen Island

Good Memories

Playing in the sand at the beach, and making sand castles with a pail.
Going out on my father's motor boat.
Playing on the Dragon at the playground.
My aunt, Pa's youngest sister and who still stayed with my grandmother, would check and clip my finger nails every time I visited.
Playing ghost house with my cousins.
Family outings to the amusement park, and riding the merry-go-round.
Pretending to take pictures of my sister using the entrance door. I'd sit on top of the shoe cabinet behind the door when it was open. I then looked through the peephole while my sister posed herself. "Ready, smile!" and I turned the door knob then quickly released it to imitate the sound of photo-taking.
Going to see the Care Bear movie.
Watching American cartoons, like Smurfs, Strawberry Shortcake, Chip n' Dale, Sylvester, and the Road Runner.

Once, my parents brought the entire family to a large open-air cinema. I remembered buying fried chicken from the snack shop before the movie started. The whole time I did not pay attention to the movie, but I absolutely loved the experience.

Li-An smiled to herself as her wrote the last good memory for the day.

The hundred and fortieth day

The good memories were the mundane things that'd skipped Li-An's recall. The bad ones were so much more dramatic, so easier to conjure. But Li-An made it a point to think of ten good ones each day so that by the fortieth day she had four hundred of them jotted down. It wasn't easy to work against the effects of the Xter pill, but at least Li-An was feeling slightly better than before. That thick coating over her head was starting to clear up and her range of vision was slightly wider than a month and half before.

Even the bad memories that came to her these days were not as painful to recall. Li-An remembered the days when her mother would chop a few shallots, and red-hot chilies and stuff them into Li-An's and her elder sister's mouths in order to quiet them down. Or how she'd open the window grill and threaten to throw them out of the thirteen-story apartment unless they stopped crying. Putting together all that the pill had made her remember, Li-An actually had a much clearer picture of her early life. She realized now that it was because her mother was lonely and helpless that she vented all her frustration on her children. But Li-An, being the more sensitive of the two sisters, took her mother's words and actions so much more seriously.

She thought about the moles. When her mother expressed disgust with the moles on Li-An's face, she began to hate the way she looked. "When I first gave birth to you, you never had moles. Now look at you, two on both your cheeks." Li-An's mother began counting the moles on Li-An's face. Five in total. But it was the two black dots located on her cheeks – one on each side – that were the most distinctive. They were located in exact alignment with and equidistant from her nose, such that Li-An was often teased by her classmates and relatives. Instead of consoling and protecting her, Li-An's mom chose to blame her daughter for the imperfections. In quiet protestation, Li-An focused on other, more attractive features like her Cupid's bow lip. She'd even look in the mirror and cover the middle part of her face with her hand so that she saw only her lips and eyes. But then one day, a black spot appeared just below her bottom left chin. Li-An's mom immediately spotted it and told her to press hard on the spot to prevent it from growing. Had Li-An not listened to her mom, no one would have taken notice of that insignificant mark. But being eighteen years old and still looking to her mother for approval, Li-An was convinced she'd turned ugly and started to pick at the black spot. She would scratch it so hard that the area started to bleed, and pus would form. Even after it healed, she would pick on the spot again and again until one day she suddenly realized she'd scarred herself. A keloid. She'd since learned to live with it.

Li-An's thoughts turned to her sister, who seemed immune to the family's turmoil. Or pretended to be, which kind of worked. Her sister didn't do well in the junior college entrance examinations, and got a place in a mediocre school near their house. Nevertheless, she managed to flourish. Member of the acting club at her new junior college. Singer at major school functions. Command leader of the student-led police squad back in her secondary school. As Li-An's sister grew in self-confidence, so did her grades. When Li-An confided in her sister how she was struggling in school, the response was a sarcastic one. "Maybe I'm more suitable than you for AAJC." Upon entering university, her sister quickly found herself a rich boyfriend. The Tan family were among Kramen Island's elite. Li-An's parents were certainly pleased. They didn't complain when her sister began spending the night at her boyfriend's place located in the heart of Kramen Island. Nasser Road, a long narrow pathway flanked by stately mansions and overpriced condominiums. The street cut into Kramen Island's main shopping district, Planter's Road, so the land on which the house stood could fetch a huge premium. Li-An's paternal grandmother kept urging Li-An's sister to marry so that she'd be all set. A university degree was unnecessary now that Li-An's sister had hooked up with the son of a manufacturing magnate.

But what disturbed Li-An the most was that her sister took after her mother in displaying her body. Li-An's sister reached puberty at an early age. By fourteen she already had large breasts. C cup. Her sister was embarrassed at first but after meeting her rich boyfriend, began showing them off. At home, she wore only a light, translucent white singlet – albeit with bra on – and shorts so short that they showed off her bum cheeks. Li-An would look at her father and tuition teacher – a male in his late twenties – for any signs of arousal if her sister happened to cross their paths. "Dress properly, will you!" Li-An's father infrequently blurted out. But her sister was defiant and stormed away. She used heavy footsteps to demonstrate her displeasure. "Let her be" was her grandmother's reply. Growing up with sexually charged parents, Li-An knew they'd lost authority with their elder daughter.

Li-An, however, grew increasingly repressed. Confused even. She knew about the secret talks between her mother and elder sister late at night. She also knew that her mother was teaching her elder sister sexual tricks. Li-An was studying late one night when she heard giggles in her sister's room. Curious, Li-An knocked on the door but seeing a small crack she opened it. "Get out! When the time comes, I'll teach you all you need to know." Her mother waved Li-An away. A year later, when Li-An did have a boyfriend, she was shocked to learn what exactly her mom was teaching her and her sister. Explicit details and steps on how to please men. The only rule set by Li-An's mom was no intercourse. Too easy. Li-An's mom had made it too easy for her daughters' pursuers. She was eager to marry them off, thinking it was the only way to survive, just as she had. But not all men were the same. While Li-An's sister did get married to her rich boyfriend, Li-An was not so lucky. "It's your bad luck. Who told you to find such a bad date in the first place" was her mom's reply shortly after Li-An was dumped by her boy-friend. Li-An was made to take the blame for everything, from her brother's death to choosing the wrong partner. Her parents were quick to turn against their own daughter when things turned out wrong. "It's a pattern and I need to break it," said Li-An as she opened her eyes and found herself soaking in the bathtub of her hotel room, her fingers all creased up. She had dozed off in her semi-consciousness state. It was a wonder that she hadn't drowned.

By the hundredth and ninetieth day, Li-An felt acute exhaustion. For weeks, she was bedridden.

"Soreness from the neck down. A tingling sensation in the head." Samantha was reading off Li-An's medical chart with the latest updates. "Good! It's the beginning of healing."

"How so?" Li-An continued to lie flat on her bed. Her face was a pale color and her voice weak.

"Transformation is taking place. Your body is now slowly releasing all the tension, all the knots. Sit up and stretch your neck to one side." ordered Samantha. Li-An stretched her neck to the left.

"How do you feel?"

"I feel a stretch on a line up to my head." replied Li-An with tired looking eyes.

"That's it! That's your lifeline. It's also a function of the pills. Good! You've been doing what I told you. Very soon you'll see results. Just hang in there." Samantha turned and headed for the door, but before making her exit, turned back uncharacteristically, and gave Li-An an encouraging wink. Li-An had no idea what Samantha meant by "your lifeline" but was too tired and weak to ask.

More weeks passed and Li-An did begin to see a positive change in her appearance. The wrinkles on the edges of her eyes had disappeared. Her cheeks were no longer sallow but supple. Her eyes glowed like those of a healthy fish. Even her hair began to look like Samantha's. Long, thick and sooty black. She'd swept her hair to the left side of her face where there were more curls. With her soft, feminine features, Li-An looked elegant but at the same time fragile. As she gained strength, she began working out at the hotel gym. Swimming too.

In a couple more months even the dreams went away. And then the coating over her brain. She felt lighter and more positive than she'd ever been in her life, as though she'd been purged. Now she was on the upward slope, they told her, but it would take months more for the drug to achieve its full effect. So best to just enjoy the resort, read, and think about the future, not the past.

And she could read again. She consumed novels by the pool like they were boxes of chocolates.

Her last year at Sentacruz was all about testing. They'd take constant samples of her saliva, blood, urine, and even small scrapings of her skin and clips of her hair. They also began talking about her "mission". Cryptically at first, as though she'd already been told what that was, but had forgotten. Something she was required to do after she left Sentacruz. And they gave her a device shaped like a tablet computer that they called a "RexPad" and told her to carry it with her everywhere and at all times. "We need to track your movements, and never be out of communication," explained Samantha. "This is just as important to your mission as the Xter pills."

"Congratulations, Julianne." said Evans one morning, who in contrast to Li-An only seemed to deteriorate with time. His face cracked whenever he talked. "We've now made you as stunning as you can be, and you'll remain that way for a good long time. There's no point keeping you here any longer. It's time to go and complete your mission."

"And what exactly is that?" asked Li-An, deep down afraid to hear the answer.

"Why, didn't we brief you? I'm sure we did. You must have forgotten during all the pain of therapy. It's to pass on your altered genes of course."

Li-An was stunned, but also embarrassed. Had they really told her this, and she'd forgotten? Deep down, she didn't think so.

"I've been able to stop your aging but not extend your fertile years. You have till forty at most. To complete the experiment, we need to see if what we've done for you will be passed on to your offspring. If you reach that age and still no offspring, you are out of the game."

As he finished the last sentence, he glanced at the RexPad she was holding in her right hand.

"That's not just to track you," he said with sudden seriousness, and obviously referring to the device.

"It's connected to your lifeline - it's an extension of you. It's to ensure that you complete your mission."

"What do you mean?" asked Li-An

"Let's hope I never have to explain," said Evans, his voice lowering to almost a whisper.

"And one more thing," he added

"Don't become like me." Evans snapped his fingers and the light moved to shine on his face.

Li-An nodded gravely, although she didn't understand. How could she possibly become like him?

"How old are you now, Julianne?"

"I just turned twenty-six."

"I've been observing you. You're different from the others who've been through here. I sense you're a very ambitious young woman. And you have ideals."

Evans paused before speaking again.

"But don't ever fall in love."

Without another word, the Professor then turned and exited through the far end of the hall.

7 AN (UN) NATURAL SELECTION

Why didn't Li-An love Grey, her fiancé? She had certainly tried, despite Evans' advice. But then love wasn't the essential element that had brought them together.

The "mission" as Samantha later revealed to her in more detail, was not only to reproduce by age forty, but choose a partner of the right haplotype group. They were to vet her choices using samples of DNA she was required to collect. It was not Li-An's intention, however, to spend her life in a marriage raising children. She would live first, she reasoned, and only cross that bridge later. She was well-fitted for an academic career, and writing a PhD dissertation would be a gift to herself; a strategy for putting off her obligation to Project X Inverted for as long as possible.

Grey was a university professor, an eminent scholar whose own dissertation had won a national prize. They met while she was doing research in Guangzhou, where he headed a nationally-prominent institute. She needed a powerful figure like Grey to open doors. Li-An sensed he was attracted to her from their first meeting in his office, but maintained a professional relationship with him through two years of moving back and forth from Kramen to China. She was then in her mid-thirties, and was enjoying life in an ageless body.

But Project X Inverted was always knocking on her door. Had she found a potential mate, they wanted to know, and what was his haplotype group? The protocol called for Li-An to send Professor Evans saliva samples of any men she might start a relationship with. She'd done that a half dozen times, but never with favorable results.

"The chemistry" for a successful relationship was literal in her case. Most possibilities had fizzled in the petri dish, though she sometimes wondered if there was any connection between the failed DNA tests and the poor character of those men she'd dated. But what could she do?

When Li-An turned 36, the lab sent her something of an ultimatum. They wanted samples more regularly to prove she was seriously dating. And this was to continue until she became engaged. It was at that moment she thought about Grey. He liked her, after all, and had status. He was certainly able to keep up his end of an intellectual conversation. Li-An started inviting him to lunch and he readily accepted. One day while he was in the wash-room she used a swab to take a DNA sample from the rim of his drinking glass, and put it carefully in her purse. When she returned home, she immediately mailed it to the lab in Sentacruz and waited for what she thought deep down would be a nil return, like the others. But not this time. Although he was Han Chinese, like Li-An, he was part of a quite different maternal haplogroup. "Congratulations!" emailed Evans, "you've found an excellent match for our purposes! Pursue him." She hadn't invested any emotions in Grey. But once he was confirmed as a positive match, she tried.

"Do you like Hangzhou?" Grey asked her one evening in their Guangzhou hotel room in a three-story house located in Dongshankou, one of the oldest neighborhoods in Guangzhou. This was Republican-period Canton, as Guangzhou used to be called. The district authorities had preserved most of the historic architecture, giving a distinctive early twentieth century character to the neighborhood. Their hotel was a converted villa, and the room she chose was on the rooftop, with an open-air balcony. There was no attached bathroom, but it did have a small outdoor basin with a tap for running water. On the balcony, bamboo rods rested overhead on metal support for airing clothes. Most were discolored from the sun and rain. A flower pot with a dried-up cactus sat on the masonry parapet. The only place to sit was a small wooden bench. On beautiful nights such as this one, Li-An and her fiancé sat there under the moon and chatted.

"Hangzhou, huh? I went there once a few years ago. It's a pretty place. Scenic. I remember the famous West Lake. Why do you ask?"

"A university there put up a job ad recently. If I apply and get the position, will you follow me there?" He paused for a moment. "It's not as reputable as the one here. But I've lived in Guangzhou for close to twenty years and feel like a change. And the benefits are attractive." He went on to explain the incentives, which included enough cash to make a down payment on a decent apartment. The salary that he drew from the institution in Guangzhou was not commensurate with his high status, and Grey was still living on the old campus in a small apartment given him under the socialist welfare housing distribution scheme.

"I'm not sure yet. Uprooting to China is a big decision to make. But it does sound like a great opportunity. You should at least give it a try," replied Li-An encouragingly, but noncommittedly. She had avoided the idea that in committing to a marriage, she was also committing to living full-time in China.

Grey wrote to Hangzhou the next day and was quickly offered the job. "Don't be happy yet," he told her. "I need to seek approval from my institution." Li-An found that weird. In Kramen Island or most parts of the world, all that was needed was a month or two's notice in advance to quit one's job. No company had any right to hold back its employees if they wanted to leave. But not in China. Grey had made the mistake of first breaking the news to a female staff member, who was distraught to think she'd now lose her patron. Kao shan. Literally "depend mountain". She brought her concern and those of his other staff members to a senior colleague, who then went to an even more senior figure, a retired centenarian who still remained influential at the university. True enough, the old man was furious that Grey, who had been one of his students and benefited from his patronage, would abandon his underlings. He called the dean to demand he reject the resignation. Thus did staff dynamics in the university play out just like in a typical Chinese family, where deference to elders was paramount.

The plot to keep him in Guangzhou would have worked had not Grey already thought of an ironclad excuse. He now declared that he was engaged to Li-An, and his fiancée's strong wish was to settle down in a new city, Hangzhou. What could he do but say yes? She might not marry him otherwise. He knew news of his remarriage would cancel out opposition. In his case, at least. Everybody including the dean was anxious to see him get hitched again. Even his elderly patron no longer had grounds to object to the resignation. Grey had played his cards well.

"I'll tell you only when it's settled," he mumbled under his breath one evening as they were taking a stroll along the famous West Lake in Hangzhou. Li-An found his comment cryptic. It was early 2016. They'd come to do a little recce of Hangzhou before picking out the neighborhood to live in. At the time, Li-An had no idea what he meant, and he wouldn't elaborate. She had to wait till the summer to find out, one night in a fancy Hangzhou hotel room which he'd purposely chosen. The upgrade to five-star hotels matched the upgrade both in his career and living standard. They were both in a good mood. He'd successfully transferred his Guangzhou hu kou (account) that afternoon for one in Hangzhou. And as for Li-An, she felt increasingly comfortable with him as a husband and mate. They toasted each other with the Australian Cabernet Sauvignon Li-An had bought at the duty-free shop back in Kramen International Airport. One glass and Li-An's face turned pink. Her head started to spin in a nice way. Her mind felt free as the wind. Coincidentally, their hotel was named Ye Feng. Wildwind. And it was here that Grey took the opportunity to come clean about his previous marriage and the secret he'd been keeping.

It turned out Grey's former wife had given birth to a second child. By accident. Out of the blue, she'd insisted that he wear no condom one night. He was hesitant at first but they were in the midst of making up after an argument, so he was inclined just then to want to please her, and she him. Instead, he got her pregnant and upended both their lives. China's one-child policy was then in force, and couples who wished to have more than one had to pay a hefty fine, which only the rich could afford. The majority made do, and a minority had another in secrecy. In Grey's case, his wife had left for England to hide her pregnancy, but when she returned a year later – together with their second child – he was so stricken with guilt and fear that he filed for a divorce.

Needless to say, Grey's major fear was losing his job, or fan wan (rice bowl) as the Chinese call it. As the leader of a scholarly institution, he was supposed to reinforce to his staff the rules laid down by the Party. Especially the one child policy. In the last four years, Grey had sacked two employees whose wives had given birth to an illegitimate second child. By then, he and his former wife had gone their separate ways, taking one child each. Still, he felt insecure. He'd be severely punished if someone in his circle found out and gave him away. He wanted to leave Guangzhou and go somewhere where people didn't know him, but without a good reason, it would only arouse suspicion if he applied to leave. Li-An, it turned out, provided that reason.

Li-An was fine with the truth. But now that he was in a new environment, free from the weight of suspicion, with even more status and pay, he began to change. While he still came across as polite and mild-mannered in public, he behaved very differently at home. He'd unexpectedly throw insults at Li-An, though he called them "harmless teases", or mere figures of speech. "See, when you marry me, you'll get half the share of my new house," he said, actually waving the title deed at Li-An's face the day he got it. Putting together everything that he'd told her, Li-An was beginning to feel like a tool he had used to plot his escape from Guangzhou. Now that he'd succeeded, the table was turned in his mind. "Look at that midriff of yours," he said on more than one occasion. The scientists back at the Sentacruz lab had certainly performed a miracle on Li-An's appearance. But it was up to Li-An to maintain her physique. At age 39, she found it challenging to keep an absolutely flat tummy. Plus Grey had an impossibly high standard. His ideal was Fan Bingbing, a top-grade Chinese movie star. "Celebrities like them pay to have a rib or two removed in order to achieve a slim waist. So that they look good onscreen and in photo shoots," he told her more than once, as though, despite her Xter-enhanced beauty, she was in need of further medical treatment to approach his ideal. And this from a man who was hardly dashing, but looked old for his age at 42. A hectic work schedule had given him an oily scalp, and within a year of their engagement, his hairline was noticeably receding, with white hairs replacing black. He was also shorter than Li-An by about two inches. Not given to exercise and body building, he looked small and frail standing or walking next to her.

She also discovered his bad temper. When aggravated, he'd holler at Li-An and even throw things. One evening, they were out on the street flagging for a cab to take them to a dinner function. Ten minutes passed and no luck. When they finally got a taxi using the fast-growing DaDa ride-hailing app, the driver lost his way. Grey tried to offer directions but it ended in a communication breakdown. A string of vulgarities blurted from his mouth, the equivalent of "Go to hell!" in Chinese, and worse. At home later that night, Li-An confronted Grey about his choice of words to the driver, while trying hard not to provoke him. He had showered and was resting comfortably on the bed next to her, while she was dressed in his favorite black silk nightgown. Silk, the trademark product of Hangzhou. The top part of the nightgown was a piece of black-colored lace with a sexy cutting. Li-An's breasts were covered, but the slightly flared edges of the nightgown– pushed out by her robust B-cup – revealed their contours. The straps crisscrossed at the back, and the only way to get out of the dress was to pull it from the bottom up. And Li-An's prominent nipples – "grape-like" was his description – stuck out through the light, flimsy material. Needless to say, he was aroused. He moved closer and started caressing her breasts.

"Will you not say those words anymore?" she asked. He claimed not to know what she meant, and Li-An explained her unease at his exchange with the taxi driver. "I didn't," he said. "But I clearly heard you," insisted Li-An. "I said I *didn't*." His voice was low but now vehement. "But I..." started Li-An, but he cut her off in mid-sentence. "How many times do I have to tell you! I did not say those words to the driver! I'm someone who detests the use of vulgar words, and here you are accusing me. I didn't! I didn't! I didn't!" He shouted at the top of his voice, as he sat straight up on the bed. "Let me recall. I called the driver. I told him to take a right at that small lane but he couldn't find it..." She tried to interrupt to calm him down. "Shhhh!!!! Keep quiet! I need to think!" He raised his voice again and this time Li-An was scared. She turned away, her back facing him, and began to quietly sob.

"Are you crying? Did I make you cry? Oh, I'm so sorry." He laid back down and hugged Li-An from behind, gently wiped her tears away. Li-An turned to face him. "I'm scared," she said. "Let's make love" was his reply. Without waiting for an affirmation, he rolled on top of her and suckled her breasts, biting so hard into one of them that Li-An let out a scream. She told him to stop but it only turned him on more. With his right hand, he grabbed both sides of the lacy top and worked them down to the center of her chest, exposing her breasts on either side. He then roughly massaged them with his other hand, one after the other, in quick circular motions. "I go crazy whenever I see your breasts," he said. Li-An had stopped resisting, which he mistook for consent. So he took off his underwear, and roughly thrust himself into her.

The next morning, they took a cab to the airport. Li-An had to catch a flight back to Kramen Island. They didn't talk. She was staring out of the window while Grey took out his phone to check his latest LetsChat postings. She decided to break the silence. "Do you know what you did last night?" Grey looked up, thought for moment and answered: "No, nothing happened last night." He looked back down on his phone and swiftly scrolled down the page with upward flicks of his finger, each flick seeming to warn her not to pursue the conversation. He was busy, his finger said, even though nothing on the screen was obviously catching his attention.

Back in Kramen Island, Li-An felt safe. She was lukewarm to his prompts on LetsChat, replying to his messages with either a cold "yes" or "no". Or an "en", the Chinese equivalent to "ok". And certainly, no more video chats. Li-An was sick of doing what they'd done when she'd gone home before: taking off her clothes in front of the camera while Grey jerked himself off. She asked herself how this had happened – the quick engagement, the equally quick change in his personality, her feeling of alienation. She began to question Professor Evans' choice of this man. If the men before him were no better and had their genes rejected, what special quality did this one have that Evans had detected in his DNA sample? But even if he matched what Evans was looking for, no one, Li-An told herself, deserved the strictures she was under, nor an endless cycle of bad experiences. There must be a way out.

Li-An had always told herself that pursuing a PhD was her way of putting off marriage, despite it having led her, in the end, to engagement with Grey. But she knew there were deeper reasons she'd taken that route, even if she couldn't fully understand them. She'd been compelled to learn certain things that weighed on her. As she lay in bed before drifting off, her thoughts turned to her research in China; the strange visions that brought her there. Visions she'd never discussed with Grey or Evans or anybody. She wondered if they somehow contained her salvation.

8 MAO'S MIRACLE

Even Li-An was shocked to discover those documents. In her first year of dissertation research in China, she'd hardly made any progress. Her professors at Kramen University had warned her: "It's a fascinating topic for a history dissertation, no doubt, but only if you can find materials." Li-An knew she was taking a huge risk. Her reading of secondary sources showed that all genetic experiments performed in early communist China had only been on plants. Not humans. And when she got to the National Library in Beijing, she found only university agriculture journals detailing botanical research. Cross-breeding of the finer breeds to improve the quality of yields or achieve growth in productivity. The earliest genetics journals that Li-An managed to find were not historical enough. She wanted materials from the Cultural Revolution. But Chinese scholars were forbidden to write about that period, while foreign scholars who attempted to were either criticized or denied archival access.

"You are not one of us. No matter how good your dissertation is, nobody in this country will believe you" was Grey's wry comment. Li-An kept silent. She needed him too much at that point to burn her bridges.

As a full professor of the history of medicine, and her informal advisor in China, Grey had turned out to be a useful contact. She only had to mention his name or produce a letter of recommendation with his signature, and any door would open. But neither Grey nor anyone in his circle knew why Li-An was pursuing

the topic "Human Genetic Research in China in the Mao Period".
As far as they knew there hadn't been any. Her statement "I'm
interested in human biological experiments" never failed to elicit
curious looks or stares from her interviewees. "Yes, I know about
Unit 731. But that's not what I'm interested in," she'd often have to
say, correcting the assumption she was researching experiments on
Chinese by the Japanese army in the puppet state of Manchukuo.
"No, it's experiments on Chinese people by Chinese scientists. In a
village. In a sphere-like structure. One that glitters day and night. It
involves organs being transferred." Li-An had blurted out this
description to a Chinese scientist she was interviewing, a 72-year old
genetics researcher. He stared at Li-An for a long time. She knew
from that look that she'd finally found the right person. "You know
about this, don't you?" probed Li-An. The old scientist nodded his
head, his gaze still fixed at her. "Go find Chief Librarian Li at
Hong'an Archives Hall." He then slowly rose from his chair and
ushered Li-An out of the office without another word, ending the
interview.

What she didn't tell him, or anyone else, was that these
descriptions of historical events and settings didn't come from
archival discoveries, but from inside her own head. Those scenes
had begun appearing in Li-An's sleep toward the end of her two-
year trial at Sentacruz. The final six months. At first, they were
snippets of images she could hardly make out. Like shots for a
storyboard flashing in front of her in disorderly fashion. Or frames
in a comic strip. And the onus was on Li-An to piece the story
together. In the first month, she assumed they were side effects from
the Xter trials, so didn't consider them significant. They always
featured the same two locations. One was a village, filled with men
and women with Asian features. They were all wearing the same
uniforms and caps. The other was a spherical structure which filled
the entire frame of her vision. They appeared like simple pencil-like
drawings initially, so Li-An didn't feel they reflected a reality. And
even as side effects, they were much more tolerable than the scenes
from her traumatic past. It was not until the second month, when
more scenes accumulated, and began flashing at a quicker rate -
around five seconds per shot - that Li-An began to think about their
possible meaning. They developed more detail over time. Men in
lab coats were conducting surgery on human patients, two at a time.

In one scene, the men in lab coats were pulling the same organ from each body. In another, they were transferring the organ from one patient to the other, in some form of even exchange. Another scene was of a huge congregation of people, who were either singing or chanting.

In the fourth month, Li-An started to see the same scenes in color. Word bubbles began to appear, inside of which Chinese characters started to form. They were talking about cells, and genes and organs, but the dialogue was all fractured and didn't make sense. She grew increasingly curious and looked forward to bedtime, when one more scene might be added to the storyboard. During the day, when she was sober, Li-An would try piecing all the scenes that'd been revealed to her into a coherent narrative. She sensed it was her task to rearrange them as if she was fixing a jigsaw puzzle. She didn't manage to make a story, but eventually, at least, Li-An understood the context. She knew she was seeing scenes of China during the Cultural Revolution. For aside from the doctors in their lab coats, others were wearing the uniforms of Red Guards. And she knew that the man in charge of it all was named Wu.

There were no new details after a while, only repeating scenes of Wu and his team of scientists at work. The last new image revealed to Li-An was one of glaring brightness. But there was nothing to indicate if it belonged at the beginning or end of the story.

After she was discharged from Sentacruz, Li-An spent days in the library reading up on China's modern history. But there was no reference to anything that resembled the scenes she'd seen. No historian of modern China had discussed mass organ transplants or experiments on human beings during the Cultural Revolution. So were the incidents she saw real? Months passed and Li-An had almost convinced herself that those graphic scenes were most likely the side effect of Evan's experiments combined with her own imagination. But they kept recurring, and insistently, as though compelling her to seek out their meaning. So when Li-An enrolled as a PhD student in Chinese history at Kramen University, and needed to pick her dissertation topic, she took the bold step of crafting it around her visions. She never revealed the source of her inspiration to her dissertation committee, of course, telling them that she was interested in the *theoretical* side of genetic research in

Mao's China. No one had written about it, she said (which was true) so it was a topic well worth pursuing.

Now, a spontaneous comment to an aging scientist, and the indiscreet response on his face, had proven her correct. She had confirmation that what she'd seen in her mind was pointing her to a buried past; a deeply hidden reality.

"Bizarre as they were, the experiments were very advanced for the time," said Chief Librarian Li of Hong'an Archives Hall, who spoke to her with none of the reticence of her other informants.

"And what does that mean?" probed Li-An, trying to hold back her excitement at finally finding someone with answers, and willing to share them.

She'd arrived in Hong'an the previous evening. Two days before she'd taken the high-speed train to Wuhan, where she spent the night at a cheap hotel near the bus station. Early next morning, Li-An set out on a bumpy journey to Hong'an. On arrival, she learnt that the county was famous for the hundreds of locals who were generals during the People's Liberation War.

"I mean by performing organ transfers. Unprecedented for the time. Even for today. Two or more people with matching profiles would undergo an exchange of the same organ. Once the surgery was complete, dormant genes would be "switched on" as they say in today's biochemical language, and the patient would feel thoroughly renewed. This advanced the field of bio-photonics by fifty years. Was way ahead of its time. But it was a state secret, and nobody knew. Only a few of us left. I've been expecting someone would come eventually. Well, it's time," Li was half-talking to himself and half-answering Li-An's question.

"Chief Librarian Li, I'm losing you. Can you start from the beginning?" Li-An took out her notebook and pen as she spoke.

His story began at the height of the Cultural Revolution. Chairman Mao had given instructions to destroy all reactionary elements and promote revolutionary ideas and activities. The young and hot-blooded Red Guards took the Chairman's order to the extreme and went on a rampage. They especially targeted university professors, many of whom had been their own teachers. "The Great Chairman Mao has given us sanction to revolt against old authority!" exclaimed the Chief Librarian, mimicking the language of Red

Guards. That part of the story was of course well known by everyone.

A Red Guard named Li Zhenqiang was a graduate student in the genetics department of Beijing University when the Cultural Revolution started, the librarian went on. He saw this as an opportunity to settle a personal score and began rallying students of genetics at major universities in Beijing. Professor Wu Dahai had given Li a failing grade in class for attacking the principles of classical genetics just before the Cultural Revolution erupted. Li was secretly drawn to Soviet biology and the theories of Trofim Lysenko, who claimed that organisms could evolve and be improved through their own action in the present, and not just through the slow process of genetic inheritance. But he was careful not to openly share the information given the Sino-Soviet split. Li also found out about an obscure foreign project called the "World of Realms", that seemed well suited to China's political climate. It was about creating self-sufficient colonies in spheres that would float in the sky. "I know that sounds crazy," said the Chief Librarian, "and I don't know anything about the source of it. But it was new, radical and sufficiently utopian to match the profile of the 'new matter' that was the catchphrase of the time. Everything was about slogans and phrases."

The librarian went on. "Professor Wu was brought in and made to kneel in front of a large crowd made up of Red Guards. He was shouted at by Li, severely castigated for teaching Mendelian genetics, which he condemned as "reactionary". The Red Guards, their right hands raised, shouted fervently in support of Li, and demanded that Wu redeem himself by working under their own direction. "You will help us create the Great China World of Realms! For Chairman Mao and all the comrades of our Great Motherland!" declared Li at the high point of the humiliating ritual. "Yes! The Great China World of Realms!" shouted a female Red Guard. Soon, the rest of the crowd shouted in unison, although none of them had any idea of what that meant.

"So what did it mean?" asked Li-An, now thoroughly caught up in the story.

"I've kept all the records," answered Li.

"Follow me."

Li grabbed a chunk of keys strung on a round metal ring, and walked out of his office. Li-An followed close behind. They went upstairs and through a door, which led to another door, this one made of what looked like solid iron. The Chief Librarian searched for the right key, inserted it into the key-hole, and unlocked the door with a loud squeak. The room was largely empty, contrary to Li-An's expectation. But in one corner were a set of identical boxes, stacked atop each other. Five of them, against which leaned an old wooden ladder. Chief Librarian Li adjusted the ladder to make sure it was steady, and used it to climb up a few steps and reach for the top box, while Li-An placed both her hands on the sides for support. "Here, take it," Li passed the box to Li-An, who held it carefully in her arms. Li-An looked down and saw that the top surface of the box had a thick layer of dust, as though it hadn't been opened for half a century. The Chief Librarian took the box from Li-An, set it down, took out a handful of documents and started laying them on the floor. Crude posters, small booklets, and bound documents with hand-written Chinese characters on the front page. When he was done with the first box, he continued with the second, then the third, and so on. Li-An looked on with excitement at the sight in front of her. An historian's dream.

When he was done with the fifth box, Chief Librarian Li turned to look at Li-An and said: "You will report to me every morning at 9 am sharp, and I will pass you this key," he brandished the key in Li-An's face. "You may not bring any of these documents out of this room. No photocopying. No scanning. They are older than you. Very fragile. You can only copy them by hand, or you may take photos with your camera. Now that you have all these materials, I expect you to do a good job with your dissertation. You understand me?" The librarian spoke with a stern voice and stared right into Li-An's eyes. "Yes, I will." As she replied, Li-An straightened her posture out of respect and gratitude. "And no need to mention me," he said on his way out the door. "Only three old people know I have these records. You met one. I retire in a year. No one will bother me about it. Good that this history is finally being written. I was worried it never would."

A year later, Li-An submitted her dissertation. Set in the Cultural Revolution, it told a story that no one outside China had previously heard, and few inside still remembered, or chose to. Professor Wu

Dahai was indeed put on trial by Red Guards led by Li Zhenqiang, a graduate student at the department of genetics in Beijing University. Li and his fellow students, many of whom Wu had taught, had first tortured him, according to a description of the event she found in Wu's own handwriting, written sometime later in the Deng period. Li was the most vicious. "Do you now plead guilty?" he'd asked while kicking Wu several times in the stomach. The professor started to cough out blood. Li also ordered a female Red Guard to shave off all his hair with a blunt knife, resulting in several cuts on Wu's scalp. Even as blood ran profusely down his face, however, Wu was determined not to give in to them, he wrote. He knew he was right. Gregor Mendel's laws of inheritance was irrefutable and the concept of genetics was key to understand human heredity. "Whose theory then do you propose I teach?" Wu quoted himself as responding, while looking up defiantly into the eyes of Li. "I will not fall for your trickery, you wily old fox!" responded Li, who must have known Wu was trying to fool him into expounding about Lysenkoism, which had been officially denounced. "Invent a new matter, or you shall perish!" shouted Li. The Red Guards followed suit. "Invent or perish!" "Invent or perish!" "Invent or perish!" At least he was not killed, thought Li-An, as many were.

In fact, Wu was even given a lab converted from an abandoned factory. His task was to help create the "Great China World of Realms", an ideal community that would be created through *biological* as well as social engineering. Extending the political evolution to human biology, after the theories of Lysenko, was apparently to be the particular innovation of this group of Red Guards. Wu could not explicitly harness Soviet models, however, but was tasked to invent an entirely new scientific paradigm in order to create an advanced Chinese worker-race. For many weeks, Wu had no idea what to do until the day when Nie Rongzhen, director of the Chinese State Science and Technology Commission, paid an unexpected visit at his factory-turned-lab. "I'm here to help you," said Nie, diving straight into the conversation without even formal greetings. "How so?" asked Wu, who by his own admission was now at his wits' end. "I've been seeing visions" was Nie's reply. "What's happening here is no accident".

Nie's vision, as he explained it to Wu, ran counter to everything known to biomedical science. He had seen human subjects undergoing an elaborate surgical process: having select organs removed and replaced by new ones from other donors. He also saw post-surgery patients experiencing some kind of a rejuvenation. Or purification. Nie wasn't sure which word to use, but observed that the patients looked cleaner, brighter, and healthier in subsequent visions. Nie was deeply suspicious of these visions at first. Organ transplant existed in the medical world, but the success rate was very low. Most patients died soon after the surgery, and why would anyone transfer the organs of healthy patients? But what if his visions were a sign, he began to think? What if they were sent to him by a higher intelligence? The visions had begun even before the Red Guards seized Wu and ordered him to 'advance human evolution'. The students may have been naively influenced by Lysenkoism. But Nie could not help but think this was all part of the same plan he'd seen in his mind. He'd learned through highly placed sources that the "World of Realm" idea had been invented in the west by a group of scientists who'd also been inspired by visions, and may be acting on them right now. It was all too coincidental. Nie decided that the only way to test the validity of what he'd seen was to perform actual experiments. One phrase he remembered being uttered in his vision was "new tissue will activate forgotten genes". He asked Wu what that could have meant.

The science of genetics, Wu said, has not been able to account for what the majority of genes do, so tended to dismiss them as useless. "So as far as the students are concerned, it is not only irresponsible, but counter-revolutionary. They think of the genes as workers, all of which have a role to play. New tissue can stimulate them, switch them on . . ."

Wu was about to criticize this reading of genetics just as Li Zhenqiang stepped through the door to the room. Li, who'd now gotten the backing of the Beijing municipal government, was even more aggressive than before. But overhearing the tail end of Wu's conversation with Nie, Li softened his tone. "Comrade Wu, I see that you've finally come around to Chairman Mao's revolutionary line. Good!" Li patted Wu on his shoulder condescendingly. "We await your blueprint." Li then introduced himself to Nie as the inspiration for this revolutionary project. But Wu noted to himself that Nie said nothing to Li of his own vision. In fact Nie lied that he'd arrived for a routine inspection. Satisfied with the answer, Li praised Chairman Mao a few more times and then retreated to the endless series of rallies and political persecutions he was now orchestrating.

Nie spent the next two days revealing his visions to Wu in elaborate detail. Wu crafted the essential points into a short document, applying the language and tone of the Cultural Revolution, including lines he had picked up while being beaten. His first paragraph began:

"Since the late Qing period, Chinese have suffered for possessing weak organs, which have made us feeble against external class enemies. Gregor Mendel would have argued that our fate is in our genes. That we are no more than what we have inherited from our forefathers. This is reactionary thought. My own research shows that there are un-activated genes in our cells that scientists from the enemy countries have neglected to understand. Without strong scientific backing, they denounced them as useless. Here, I again emphasize that this line of thought is anti-revolutionary. I announce that each and every gene can be turned on and made useful. More than that, each and every cell will be so renewed and those partaking in the experiment I propose will find their true selves. But for that to happen, we need a surgical procedure to transfer some of our organs between us. Following the proven theories of organo-therapy and tissue therapy, this introduction of new tissue will naturally regenerate the other cells in our bodies. And the exchange of tissue will make us one with each other in body as well as mind. We will even build a special structure for the purpose of living as a biological community – a sphere - whose design will itself create an energy field that will protect everyone from harm as we carry out this procedure. This way a new and superior species of the Chinese worker-race will emerge to advance the Revolution, and beyond that, create The Great China World of Realms!"

Following Nie's vision, as narrated by Wu in his hand-written memoir, a model community or village of a few hundred people would be organized for the project, and called Organville. A sphere-like structure was to be located in the middle of the village. It would be formed from gold-plated discs as described in Nie's vision. Each disc was to be of an identical dimension, and when interlocked, would form what a western engineer had dubbed a "geodesic sphere". Inside the structure would stand a crystal globe on which light shone from a glass opening at the roof. Everything inside the sphere, from walls to support columns to even the floor, would be made of white marble slabs.

On the night they finished the blueprint, entirely based on Nie Rongzhen's visions, Wu was still troubled by unanswered questions. Wu had a few times tried asking Nie what would happen when the sphere had been built and the organ exchanges performed, but each time he only deflected the question or stared up at the stars. "Comrade Nie, don't you think it's time to tell me the whole story?" Wu finally asked. "What do you mean?" Nie's eyes were glued to the report. "The aftermath. What did you see happening after it's built?" Wu's question was followed by a long pause. "I saw human society perfected," Nie answered matter-of-factly. "But what's perfection? By who's standard?" Wu asked. Nie cryptically pointed his right index finger up toward the sky. The next day, Wu handed the final blueprint to Li Zhenqiang.

The report was greeted with enthusiastic fervor by Li and his Red Guard unit, who immediately went to work on building the village and its centrally-located sphere. Most bizarrely, Chinese who were not Red Guards, nor members of the elite, began spontaneously arriving to help build and populate the utopian community. They were of many ages and backgrounds, and from many parts of China. But they were not random visitors. It turned out that each been drawn to the experimental village by their own visions. Nie had also predicted this would happen, and had reported it to a skeptical Wu on their first night together. But by now, Wu was no longer skeptical. After a long and elaborate process of bodily examination, Wu confirmed that none of the newcomers – who would eventually number in the hundreds - had ever had a disease related to an internal organ, and, more amazingly, they all had the same blood type. There was thus nothing that would prevent their becoming subjects of the planned surgery. For both Nie and Wu, this confirmed that some higher force had sent them there. In fact the newcomers included surgeons and nurses, who were easily enlisted to assist in the transplants. The two scientists pushed forward with renewed determination.

When the surgeries had been completed, and without incident, changes began happening in the village. The patients/villagers became noticeably happier, laughing and smiling to each other. Nie and Wu thought they also looked younger and more radiant than when they'd first arrived. Rumors by this time had reached elements of the party leadership in Beijing, and stories began to circulate of miracles taking place in Organville, which were invariably ascribed to following Chairman Mao's teachings. An older woman who'd been barren all her life was finally pregnant and gave birth to a healthy baby boy. A fat woman in her thirties who never had a spouse because of her weight issue, woke up one morning to find herself looking beautiful and slender. She was married within a month. A man who lost a limb from fighting in the war was even said to have grown back his leg, although that story was almost certainly apocryphal. The Red Guards themselves certainly believed that Wu's experiments had worked and that a scientific revolution was underway. But Nie and Wu ascribed the changes not just to the surgery, but to an energy field that had somehow been generated by the sphere.

Then one morning in July 1976, just two months before Chairman Mao died, Beijing woke up to find that Organville had vanished. For days leading up to its disappearance, the area was awash in light. It was summer, and the Beijing air was hot and suffocating. City folk were sitting out and fanning themselves, when suddenly a bright light shone from the horizon. Everyone knew the light was coming from the direction of Organville, but no one dared go near it. According to the official records that Li-An consulted, the experimental village had simply dissipated due to "social turmoil", as had so many "new matters" during Cultural Revolution. This was almost certainly the language of cover-up, she thought, but records of what happened had been so thoroughly expunged that the trail was left entirely cold. Two months later Chairman Mao died. Some began to interpret the village's disappearance as an omen, a sign warning of the impending death of the Great Leader. Organville was thereafter seen as bad luck, in the same category as the more infamous Tangshan earthquake, and hence expunged from official mention.

Li-An's examiners were both shocked and impressed by her dissertation. Some couldn't bring themselves to fully believe that a story like this, which bordered on fantasy, had been shielded for so long from the historical record. But then again, Li-An had the evidence to support her claims, at least about the construction of the village, the experiments conducted there, and the intentions of those who carried them out, if not what happened to it in the end. She even had actual dialogues – after Li-An had exhausted the written documents, Chief Librarian Li handed her a cassette tape with Wu's first-hand account. This all resulted in a compelling historical manuscript that read just like a novel, though one bordering on science fiction. Word soon got out to the publishing industry and major American university and trade presses began pursuing Li-An with attractive book contracts.

But Li-An was left unsettled by the experience. Her research had proven that the comic drawings she saw in her sleep were not side effects of her drug therapy, but recorded actual events. Events which only revealed themselves many years later in an obscure Chinese county archives hall. But why her? What were the connections? She was left with a lingering feeling that what she'd just discovered was somehow connected to her fate.

14

9 GLIMPSES OF A PAST

Completing her dissertation had halted Li-An's visions from the Cultural Revolution, which now became documented scenes in a history book. She wondered if they ever would have ended had she not sought out their reality. But there were still other scenes that would play in her mind from time to time, glimpses of a past that she suspected were her own, but that she couldn't remember with any clarity. One image that kept surfacing was that of a full-bearded man reaching out to hold the hand of a woman sitting across from him at a desk. Behind the man were shelves of books, so Li-An figured they were in his office. He was older than the woman, who had the body of a young adult, and might or might not be her. Li-An could only see her from behind.

Another image was more dramatic. Blood. Lots of blood, and Li-An could almost smell that strong, metallic odor whenever the scene came up. The same bearded man was franticly running in and out of Li-An's vision like she was watching a movie. He'd enter with a fresh towel, bent over to look at Li-An who obviously was taking the perspective of whoever was bleeding, dabbed constantly at stained sheets, and exited the scene. Yet another scene: the same man on all fours and moving back and forth, obviously having sex with the same woman from previous scenes. But this time he looked angry and when he came, pulled out with force before uttering "You bitch!" It was a scene devoid of tenderness. There were many more. But Li-An could never piece those snippets of images together to create a coherent picture. All she knew was it was always the same bearded man and woman, and despite the violence, Li-An could feel a strong, blissful bond between them.

10 VIDEO-CHAT

13th January 2017, 7.02 pm

"Li-An, where are you?"

13th January 2017, 7.07 pm

"I miss you, especially now. 2017.1.13 Night 19:07."
White had written the time and date – in the typical Chinese order of year, month, and day – in order to mark the moment as special.

13th January 2017, 7.56 pm

"Ha Ha," Li-An replied. She'd just gotten out of the shower when his text arrived. She added a smiley face with eyes closed, and two tints of red on the cheeks below both eyelids. But Li-An was more amused than embarrassed by his declaration of affection.
"Where are you now?" he asked.
"Back in Kramen Island. But I'm scared of good-looking men with sweet mouths," Li-An wrote back.
"You call this sweet mouth? I'm just expressing how I feel. When are you coming to China next?"

"But you were so quiet in Beijing. Not sure when I'm coming again." Li-An honestly had no plans of returning to China except to marry.

"I'm thin-skinned." White added the same rosy-cheeked emoticon that Li-An had used previously.

"And you already have a girlfriend," she reminded him.

"I'm no good with words." White was still replying to Li-An's comments about his reticent behavior at the Beijing restaurant.

"So you're the type that acts rather than talks?" Li-An quipped.

"I do, to speak the truth." Was he responding to her girlfriend comment, or her suggestion he was a public introvert? The rhythm of LetsChat often created ambiguity.

13th January 2017, 8.01 pm

"And what type are you?" asked White.

"The sexy type," replied Li-An, following the message with a grinning emoticon. She knew she'd crossed a bridge. But what harm could it do? She was in the mood to tease.

"Yes, you are," he wrote back

"Come take a picture. I want to see your sexiness."

She hadn't expected he'd take the bait, so immediately regretted her comment. He'd been so awkward at the restaurant.

"I saw that intimate picture of you and your girlfriend the night in the plane when you took out your cellphone," she replied. "And you still had the cheek to ask me out?"

"Why? What's wrong with that?" he wrote back without pause, adding an innocent-looking face to give license to his reckless behavior. All the features were rounded, from the eyes to the pupils to the mouth. Even the hands flanking the face were Doraemon-esque. There was a little black question mark close to one eye.

"I'm not that easy," Li-An replied.

"Me neither."

"Not faithful though."

He replied with another smiley. Both arms were raised, the right one higher than the left in almost Taiji-style fashion, signaling an attempt to deflect criticism.

"Let's just be friends," Li-An wrote, followed by a grin.

"No, couldn't you tell I was just shy that night? We are too far apart. In two countries."

"Otherwise, we could get to understand each other better."

"Take a picture for me," he asked a second time.

Li-An was having difficulty figuring him out. Why so shy in person and bold on LetsChat? And why all the emoticons? Now she was starting to use them too, which she'd never done before.

13th January 2017, 8.13 pm

"I'm glad you're shy actually. That night I was worried that you'd follow me to my room. And there are pictures of me on LetsChat already. I don't know you well enough.
"

13th January 2017 8.14pm

"Xiao Yang Ba Ni," responded White. Li-An didn't understand his Northern China slang. She would find out later on the Chinese search engine Baidu that Xiao Yang was a common phrase for teasing the opposite sex, but was almost without meaning.

"You didn't even invite me up to your room. You had things to do, no?" White remembered the lie that Li-An told at the Beijing restaurant to escape dinner early.

"Our meeting that night was too brief, don't you think so?"

His persistence began to impress her. But who was this person?

13th January 2017, 8.39 pm

"So you're attracted to me?" wrote Li-An. This time, she added not a face but a hand with the forefinger sticking out like it was hooking for an answer.

"What do you think?"

"I think you're attracted to my butt. You saw it in the plane when I was sleeping."

"Really?" denied White.

"My coat is big. You were fully covered in it. What's more, all the lights were out that night in the plane."

"The next morning. When the plane landed, and I stood up, I saw you watching me." Li-An clearly remembered him checking her out as she turned and walked for the exit.

"I was concerned for you. Worried you might get a cold." White had used the Chinese expression aixin fanlan. Transliteral meaning: "flooded with love".

"I'll tell you what we are. We are fated to meet but not destined to be together. Just find me in your dreams. It's impossible. The two of us."

"There's no such thing as an absolute yes or no. It's all about you and how you think, no?" replied White.

"As you said, we're just too far apart," Li-An quickly replied.

13th January 2017, 8.49 pm

"Do you absolutely have to think this way?" he wrote back.

"Plus, you already have a girlfriend," she replied.

"Let's enjoy chatting here first and when the opportunity comes, we'll meet. Isn't that good?" suggested White.

"Just remember not to call my name out when you make love to her," replied Li-An teasingly. She'd added an icon of a penguin wrapped in a red scarf and walking, airily, its wings spreading out.

"Confident girl, aren't you?"

"But you like that, no?"

"Never thought you can be such a teaser."

"Have I gotten you excited?" Li-An quipped.

"Are you at home?" he asked.

"I know what you want. Forget it."

"What?" (emoticon with a question mark on the top right hand of its head, eyes a full rounded shape and slanted more to the right)

"You jolly well know," responded Li-An.

"You think too much, Li-An," he replied.

Li-An was surprised at how much she was enjoying herself. At how frank she wanted to be with someone she'd not even liked when they'd met face to face.

13th January 2017, 9.13 pm

"Just fantasize making love to me in your sleep tonight," she chanced.

"First, snap a picture for me."

"No."

"Fu Le" (I give up). Then, let's go to bed. If you encounter any interesting things or people, share with me. Sweet dreams." White added an emoticon that was falling asleep, with a long trail of Z's.

Li-An replied with an emoticon waving goodbye. She'd meant it to be forever.

A week passed. She found herself missing the playful exchange she'd had with White. The LetsChat White was not the plane-and-restaurant White. She liked him better this way. So why not continue? She wouldn't fall in love, she told herself. They'd never actually meet again. She'd just pretend to be as young as he thought she was. She'd be as young inside as Xter pills had made her look outside. It'd just be for fun.

Li-An found White again on LetsChat.

21st January 2017, 10.08 pm

"Lunar New Year's around the corner. How have you been?"

"Li-An!" he replied almost immediately.

"What are you doing?"

"About to go shower."

"How have you been the past week? Take a picture. I want to see you."

"You first, then me," answered Li-An.

Why did men always ask for photos, she wondered? Pictures of both of them were already all over their LetsChat pages. She didn't need his, so wasn't sure why she agreed. Was she worried he'd lose interest?

A photo of White quickly filled her screen. He was holding his cellphone up with his left hand in front of a mirror, dressed in a grey-colored coat, his hair neatly gelled up. He looked attractive in the photo. Manly. Suave. More so than she remembered from their two meetings. Maybe photos were a good idea after all, she thought. He'd taken that one exclusively for her, but then again, had he? Maybe it was already in his phone.

"Gege, you look so smart!" Gege. Big brother. Li-An decided she'd address White this way to create the illusion that he was older. It made her feel more like the young woman she appeared to be.

"Beijing is too cold now. How's the weather in Kramen Island? Are you sweating a lot?"

No one talked about weather on Kramen Island. It was always just hot.

21ˢᵗ January 2017, 10.50 pm

A picture of Li-An appeared on their message board. She had just finished her shower and took a selfie in the bathroom. She'd angled the phone towards her right and slightly above eye level. She made sure not to include the mirror lest the camera capture her naked body. But she purposely revealed a small fraction of her right breast.

"Xiao Yang," White replied almost instantly.

21ˢᵗ January 2017, 10.55 pm

"You finished washing yourself? Xihao La," a phrase referring to the woman washing herself especially her private parts before sex. White was obviously stirred by Li-An's photo.

21ˢᵗ January 2017, 11.03 pm

"What's the meaning of Xiao Yang?" Li-An couldn't help but ask. This was the second time White had associated her with this term.

"I am Xiao Yang. I am like this. That's the meaning."

"Yes, exactly! That's me! I love to tease," she wrote back.

"Do you find this fun?"

"Not bad. It's late. Not sleepy?" he asked.

"I am."

"Then, go to bed. We'll talk again. If you come across anything interesting or fun, share with me. Remember." (an emoticon with tongue sticking out)

"Find me during the New Year, Big Brother."

"Hao Di" (Ok)

27th January 2017, 10.07 pm

"What are you doing, Li-An," White wrote.
It was 27th January 2017. Chinese New Year Eve. He had kept his promise.

27th January 2017, 10.22 pm

Again, Li-An had just gotten out of the shower when she saw his text. She pondered over how to reply, but in the end decided to just send him a picture of herself. It was what he was always asking for. She went through her gallery of photos, and chose one of herself in a one-piece silky blue pajama. Thinly strapped, Li-An's breasts were lightly covered with black lace. Her nipples were slightly visible underneath that see-through material. The top half of the pajama was held together by only one button between her cleavage, and below it was a slit extending to her belly button. She had taken the picture for her fiancé more than a year ago, upon his request.

"Sexy beautiful lady," was White's reaction.

She decided to let herself get caught in the moment.

"I want to make love to you so badly," she wrote, not really meaning it. But she felt the thrill of teasing a man who couldn't touch her.

"Take a full view of yourself for brother to see," White urged.

"No."

Minutes passed and White didn't follow up with a reply. She thought he'd lost interest.

27th January 2017, 10.30 pm

"How do you feel about me? Be honest," probed Li-An.

"Not bad," was White's weak reply.

"Hey, I'm waiting for your picture."

"Really? no."

"So wear your clothes and take a picture."

"You didn't answer me."

"I'll know only after we've tried each other out."

"You mean having sex?"

"You are too straightforward, Li-An," White replied.
"Take a picture."

27th January 2017, 10.44 pm

"Big brother, do you think about me before you sleep?"
"Yes," he replied almost instantly.
She didn't care if it was true.
"Still waiting for a photo."
"I think about you too. The past few nights."
"I'm really waiting for your photo."
Why this obsession with pictures? Wasn't chatting stimulating enough?
"I don't know how to take a full view of myself." Li-An was speaking the truth. Until now, she'd only taken selfies of herself from the chest up.
"Xiao Yang."
"Why not you first," Li-An challenged him back. Very soon White sent a picture of himself showing off his packs.

27th January 2017, 10. 50 pm

"Now your turn," he demanded.
"Promise me that you wouldn't show the picture to others if I send it. Otherwise, I'll hate you."
"Of course I wouldn't. Why would I show our stuff to anybody?"
"Za Liang'er". Us. It was the first time Li-An encountered this Northern slang. She liked it.
"Wait," she replied.
"You are the best," White added a hug expression. An emoticon with a body dressed in green.

27th January 2017, 10. 55 pm

Li-An took a picture of herself using the full-length mirror in her bedroom. She was dressed in a purple nightgown. She held the cellphone in such a way that her right arms blocked the view of her breasts. Her head was slightly tilted to the right, so the left side of her long voluminous hair clung to her face. Li-An was not looking

101

straight at the mirror but into her cellphone. She did not smile, so appeared forlorn, but in an alluring way. She pressed 'send'.

"You are damn sexy. Take a few more. Your nightgown looks good."

"Thank you."

"Take a few more for me. A side view."

"You're too greedy, Big Brother." She really wanted to stop. The photos seemed to be melting the physical distance she had wanted to maintain. And putting him in control.

"I just want to see you." He added an emoticon with droopy eyes and hands resting on chin, two fingers (one from each hand) sticking out and touching at the lip.

27th January 2017, 11.05 pm

"I knew when we met in Beijing that you wanted me," she wrote.

"I wish to see your pictures."

"Don't toy with me."

"No, I wouldn't. I'm not that kind of person."

Li-An sent another picture of herself. It wasn't too different from the first one.

"How about one with a side view?"

"I don't know how to do that."

"Take it from your side."

Again she stood in front of the mirror. This time with her body in profile, and her head turned 90 degrees to face her reflection. Her eyes still looked down on the cellphone screen at her own image. Her waist looked smaller and her shoulders even broader in that twisted position.

"It's enough. Too many photos already," texted Li-An.

"You are damn sexy."

"What do you want to do now?" To her surprise, she was highly aroused.

"Missing you," was the man's reply.

"Simply missing you," he repeated.

"I want to be taken by you," she wrote.

"I like to watch you," he replied.

"Take a short video of yourself."

"No, it's enough."

"Up to you. I'll respect your decision," she wasn't expecting him to surrender. And realized she didn't want him to.

"I want to say sexual things to you." she wrote.

"Go ahead."

"Are you hard now?"

"What do you think?"

"I bet you are. Touch me then."

"Let's video chat," he wrote. Li-An was turned on by his use of "za liang'er", meaning "let's".

"No. I'm scared."

"I'm alone now. There's nothing to be scared about."

27ᵗʰ January 2017, 11.30 pm

"I still don't think it's a good idea." She wasn't being coy now, but was truly conflicted. She was highly turned on, but didn't want to leave the medium of chat with photos for something even closer to reality.

"Don't you want to see me?" he wrote.

"Bai Xiang, come inside me." She was still enjoying the text. A fantasy of just words. He wasn't, however.

"I'm going to call you now."

"But I'm scared."

28ᵗʰ January 2017, 11.35 pm

After a brief pause, she relented. "Ok, but give me a minute." She pulled out from the drawer the blue silky slip-on pajama she wore in the photo she'd sent earlier, and quickly changed into it. Back in bed, she stacked her two pillows atop each other and placed her cellphone on them and against the bed headstand.

The phone rang.

"Big Brother," Li-An greeted White with a nervous smile. He was lying flat on his bed, his head leaning upright against the wall. His bed had no headboard.

"Oh, you changed your pajama."

"By the way, where's your girlfriend?"

"She's gone back to spend the New Year with her family." Many Chinese with city jobs had to travel long distances to see their families. A situation unlike Kramen Island, which was one-hour drive from end to end.

"And why didn't you go home?"

"I just decided not to this year."

"So you're staying in the company's dormitory?

"No, my brother-in-law's house."

"Where are they?"

"They've gone to eat reunion dinner."

"Why didn't you go with them?"

"I drank too much this afternoon. My stomach's not feeling too good."

Chinese New Year in mainland China meant "Da chi da he". Transliteral meaning: "Big Eating, Big Drinking."

"Do you want to see me?" Her fingers were fiddling with the one button securing her pajama top.

He nodded.

"But you can't take photos," Li-An demanded, her face suddenly looking stern.

"I wouldn't. Don't worry," he replied.

Li-An placed her fingers back on the button, but paused again.

"Ahhhh! You really have to promise me you'll not take photos!" Li-An made her voice sound child-like.

"No! I'm not! There's no such function anyway!" The man laughed as he responded.

"Li-An, come. Do it."

Slowly, she loosened the button and pulled the pajama top down to her waist. Li-An looked away from the camera but saw from the corner of her eyes that White, clearly affected by her naked body, let out a breath and dropped the arm that wasn't holding the cellphone. Embarrassed, Li-An looked down at the pillows while he stared on. "Bai Xiang..." Li-An called out his name a half-minute later, breaking the awkward silence. He coughed to recompose himself, reached out for a burning cigarette and took a puff. Li-An put her pajama back on.

"Did you like what you saw?" Li-An asked, her eyes looking down but watching White nodding his head from the corner of her eye. "Do you want to see it again?" she asked. "Hao." A strong, definite yes enhanced by his deep husky voice. Again, Li-An undressed, but this time looked him straight in the eye. "Fondle your right breast," he said. She did as she was told. "Now your left." "Now both together." "Stand up and remove your pajama." Li-An followed his instructions with mock-hypnotized obedience. "Turn around for me to see". "Stand further back," White ordered. "Turn around." Li-An made a 360-degree turn. By now he was fully aroused, and no longer resting on his pillow but sitting bolt upright. "Now I want to see you from the side." Li-An showed him her left side. Slowly, she returned to face the screen and White laid back down in bed. She smiled at him, and he smiled back. "You sexy beautiful little girl." Li-An liked the word "little". "You've successfully bewitched me." He pointed his right index finger at Li-An, who noticed a multi-tiered gold ring on his middle finger.

"I want to see you down there."

"No," Li-An gently shook her head in protest, her eyes looking down in embarrassment.

"Come on. Let me see you there." Again she refused.

"Let me see you first," she retorted. White lifted the blanket to reveal his red underwear but quickly covered it back.

"It's embarrassing," he said, smilingly.

"And it's not for me?" she asked.

"Li-An, come on," his voice was so stern and persistent that she finally gave in.

"Bring your phone down a bit more. Yes. Touch yourself." She did as he asked, and let out a pleasurable moan. But then quickly brought the phone up to see the man face-to-face. As she did so, she saw White sticking his tongue out as though trying to lick her. She was amused.

"Xin Nian Kuai Le". "Happy New Year". The clock above Li-An's bed struck twelve. It was the day of Chinese New Year.

"Xin Nian Kuai Le", he greeted back.

"I think I've fallen in love with you," he said.

"But this is not love," she replied.

"What I mean is . . . it's everything. Your voice, your hair, your smile . . ." he explained. "You'll find I'm a good man."

"What's a good man?" she asked, not actually caring about his answer.

"Gege, I want it." Li-An was shocked at herself for so spontaneously expressing her desire. She wasn't teasing anymore. It was real this time.

"You're wet," he said matter-of-factly.

Li-An nodded.

"And so you want."

Li-An nodded again.

"Come, put your cellphone down there." Li-An did as was told.

"Now, touch yourself." Li-An started to do as he asked but then heard a sound in the distance. It came from White's side. Like someone opening a door. She saw him hiding his erect penis with the blanket and turning his phone away from the door. Likewise, she quickly aimed her own cellphone towards the ceiling.

"How are you feeling now?" said a male voice. It must have been his brother-in-law.

"I'm ok," he replied. A few more words followed by the door shutting.

White turned back to Li-An, embarrassed. "It's late. Go to bed. I'll talk to you again."

"Ok. Good night," replied Li-An.

28th January 2017, 12.14 am

"I enjoyed it so much," wrote Li-An on their message board soon after she'd shut down their video chat.

"It's what I've been wanting," she added.

She wanted that feeling, of being wanted and wanting him back, to last as long as she could stand it.

11 THE CONFRONTATION

"What do you mean you've fallen in love?"

Evans looked up from the thick, bound document he was flipping through. Li-An could only assume he was staring directly into her eyes. There was no spotlight this time, as he wasn't in the laboratory. They were meeting in Evans' private residence, the Presidential Suite at the top of the Sentacruz resort hotel. Nevertheless, the curtains were drawn shut to keep the daylight out. The suite was as dimly-lit as the laboratory. Li-An could only roughly make out the apartment's interior, which was done up in elaborate Art Deco style. But Evans' expression completely eluded her, for he had now taken to wearing a veil over his face.

Just as she was about to answer, Evans stood up from the armchair and reached for his walking stick. Li-An noticed the odd design of the cane, which had a snake coiling around the staff. And as he walked across the hall to the bar, she saw that his gait was much slower than a decade before, which was the last time she'd seen him in the flesh. He reached for the half-filled decanter and pulled out the stopper with painstaking effort. His hand shook as he poured the whisky into the glass. His physical degeneration hadn't been obvious to her when they'd communicated over the RexPad, after she'd left Sentacruz. But FAME's firm and assertive voice certainly belied his enfeebled body.

"What do you mean you've fallen in love?"

Evans repeated his question after taking a sip of the whisky. He spoke with a crispness that meant he was ready to challenge her. So she knew she had to be careful.

"His name is White, and I've come to ask for your blessing. I don't have his DNA profile yet, but I'll send it to you as soon as I meet him again," Li-An's voice quivered as she spoke.

"Do you know the implications of what you've just said?" replied Evans, whose voice was louder than before.

"Yes, I do," replied Li-An, though not sure if they were on the same page.

A long silence ensued.

"I was once in love," he said unexpectedly. He pointed with the walking stick to a photo resting on the mantelpiece beside the bar. Kramen Island was on the equator, but the hotel had nevertheless created a fireplace for ornamental purpose, assuming it to be an essential feature of a luxurious world-class suite. Li-An went to take a closer look and saw that it was a photo of a white woman with long auburn hair.

Li-An detected a sudden softening in Evans' voice. She couldn't see his face but believed its expression too must have changed. Evans' admission made him seem more human to Li-An and she began to relax.

"Who is she?" Li-An dared a question.

"My wife," Li-An thought she heard a quiver in FAME's voice.

"She was not only my wife. She was my muse, soulmate, and my very first human subject," continued FAME.

"Your human subject? For this project?" Li-An could not contain the surprise in her voice.

"Li-An, your time is running down. Forget about love. It will destroy you. I warned you about that a long time ago, didn't I?" Evans' voice shifted back to his familiar authoritative tone, determined to change the subject back to her.

"Yes, you did. But why does it have to destroy me?" Li-An was determined to challenge him.

"Why can't love revive me? I've been dead for God knows how long. I need this. I need this to give me hope. I've never had passion, happiness . . ." She stopped to grope for words.

"All the good feelings I need to survive *your damn project*!" Starting to lose control of her emotions, she quickly stopped.

"Feelings?" Evans raised and pointed his walking stick at Li-An, his right hand supporting on the mantelpiece.

"You come to lecture me about feelings. Do you know what I had to do to erase . . ." Evans stopped in mid-sentence as though checking himself from revealing a secret. But it was too late.

"You erased things from my memory, didn't you?" Li-An was now reminded of the other reason she'd come to see him.

"Those dreams . . . nightmares . . . those . . . I don't even know what you call them anymore. Those terrible memories that kept winding through my head. That was only half of it, wasn't it?" But Evans kept silent.

"Answer me," demanded Li-An firmly. She was determined to get the truth.

"I put your mind in order. Don't make me do it a second time" said Evans, before quickly changing the subject.

"You know if you don't complete the mission, they may kill you. Because they can't trust you with this secret. And I won't be able to prevent it."

He pointed his right index finger over Li-An's head. She turned and saw behind her a built-in shelf with accent lighting over it. There were no books, only transparent boxes made from an acrylic-like material. In each box was a silvery-white slim tablet identical to the RexPad she'd been issued before she left Sentacruz. They looked like organs stored in canopic jars. The side of the box facing her – like the spine of a book – had gold imprints. Li-An walked closer and saw they were names of all fifty human trial subjects.

She found hers at the topmost rack, sandwiched between two boxes that had an additional mark, a red wax seal with the alphabet C in gothic font. In fact, all the boxes except hers were embossed. Li-An knew what the letter stood for. C for Completed. All of Li-An's compatriots had accomplished their missions save for her and their files were sealed. Her case was the only one still open.

"The RexPad is connected to your lifeline. I told you that when you left Sentacruz. They not only track you with it, they can use it to turn you off as well."

"But why can't I complete my mission with someone else," pleaded Li-An.

"I don't love the man you chose for me. I'll suffer the rest of my life if I marry him. And I certainly don't want to have his child! I'll give you anything to let me have my freedom back. I want the freedom to choose who I sleep with, who I eat with, who I fall in love with, who..." Li-An went on and on with increasing speed.

"Li-An, it's no use. This is your fate. The chances that his DNA is acceptable to us are slim. You know that from all the rejections. You'd be taking too much of a risk, leaving the one we've approved for you. And whom *you* chose. Anyway, there's just no time." Li-An roughly made out in the dim setting that FAME was shaking his head as he talked.

"I'm sorry, Professor. I don't mean to be trouble. You've done an incredible job on me, I know. I'll always be grateful to you for what I am now," Li-An said with all sincerity.

"But the price I have to pay for this, marrying him only for the sake of DNA. And what's in his DNA that you're looking for, anyway? What's so special about Grey?" she said, using her nickname for her fiancé. Evans had never heard it, but she knew he'd catch the meaning.

"His phenotype doesn't add up to anything particularly desirable" interrogated Li-An, "so what is it about his genes that appeals to you so much?"

"You don't know enough for me to explain it," replied Evans.

"Stop this you-know-nothing bullshit!" She was startled by her own boldness.

"I went to get a PhD so we could talk one day on more equal terms. I'm not that little girl anymore. I know you're brilliant. The top molecular biologist of your time. But you also have very questionable ethics. You've gotten away with it because you've had the backing of pharma companies and the government. But now you're threatening me like a gangster. It's my life! You owe it me to tell me the truth," Li-An spoke with assertive confidence.

Evans remained silent.

"I know now you were trying to 'turn off' my past traumas, because they might be expressed epi-genetically. That's what revisiting my childhood during the clinical trial was all about, no? You wanted a pool of human subjects who would not pass on trauma to their offspring. Aren't I right?" challenged Li-An.

"And it worked, didn't it?" Evans broke his silence.

"No, you don't know yet," Li-An spoke with a confidence based on years of reading on genetics and epigenetics during her PhD candidature.

"You tried to avert all possible side effects by not touching the germline. Forget mutations and all the other problems your competitors are trying to solve. You came up with the idea of inverting the entire chromosome so that everything remained intact. You were way ahead of your time, and still are. But a decade on, and you still can't publish your work, or really be certain of anything. And why is that?" Li-An paused, hoping Evans would start to engage with her, but he stayed tight-lipped.

"It's because you can't be sure what you really did to us. If we're thoroughly cleansed of our pasts." Li-An pointed to the shelf with the encased digital tablets, containing all the collected data on Evans' fifty human subjects.

"And unless you've successfully erased our memories, our traumas will be passed onto our offspring, and maybe even magnified. That's why you need us to reproduce, and the uncertainty has you worried." Evans, who until now was staring blankly in the air, turned to look in Li-An's direction.

"So you think you've figured me out, huh? You don't know the half of it." he replied.

"What I want is simple. To be with the man I love. I'm not necessary to the completion of your experiment, and I won't tell anybody about it. Let me go." pleaded Li-An.

"You call it The Lab of Possibilities. Surely, you can think of something. There must be a way out." Li-An turned to face the shelf again.

"Look at all these . . . these . . . these specimens!" Li-An thought the word "specimen" was the best description she could use to describe the people whose files were lined up like test tubes.

"You have forty-nine completed missions. One more is not going to make a difference to your research. Just let me go." Li-An pleaded.

"I would if I could. But I can't," spoke Evans matter-of-factly.

"Except . . ." he continued but stopped short of completing his sentence.

"Except what?" Li-An probed eagerly.

"I read your dissertation," FAME pointed to the thick, bound document he'd been holding when Li-An entered his suite. Li-An wasn't surprised, though he'd never bothered to mention it before.

"Mao's Miracle," FAME recited aloud the dissertation title.

"A miracle, indeed." He let out a laugh.

"You're being cryptic," responded Li-An.

"It's still there you know. Not the physical structure, but its energy field."

"You've lost me professor."

"You did a good job, Li-An. You deserve your degree. But you didn't find the full story. Go see Professor Wu. They didn't tell you, but he's still alive. And he might be able to help you," instructed Evans.

"But first sit down, and let me tell you some things about The World of Realms. Things you completely missed, but need to know."

Li-An was stunned to realize that Evans and her dissertation topic were somehow entangled. Why hadn't he revealed that across all these years? Suddenly her suspicions about Sentacruz, the visions, Organville, and her own early life all being connected, if not fated, seemed closer to being true. She lowered herself into the nearest armchair, and listened with increasingly rapt attention as Evans told his story.

12 THE WORLD OF REALMS

It was the early 1970s. Many revolutionary, even utopian, ideas were 'in the air'. But this was literally the case when a group of scientists from various fields came together to exploit what they initially termed "The In-Between". They meant the five layers of the atmosphere sandwiched between Earth and the beginnings of Space. The leader of the project was none other than Evans himself, then a promising young geneticist, and heir to a Welsh mining fortune. His circumstances allowed him to fund his own lab, in Dublin, where he lived with his Irish wife, Marianne. What if he could turn the earth's atmosphere into a habitable space, he thought? A series of communities in and above the clouds where groups of like-minded humans could live happily free from earthly concerns. And instead of creating a system of governance modeled on nation-states, which were random collections of disparate people, each realm would be inhabited by humans chosen for their like-mindedness. To Evans, all the sufferings on planet earth were the result of conflicting human beliefs and ideologies. Wars and exploitations of all kinds happened because of perceptual differences, and could only be corrected if like-minded people created their own little worlds.

This concept was hardly new. Evans was one of a long line of utopian thinkers. What was new about his scheme was locating it in the air. Making communities completely independent of the ground; a new start in the long, sad history of earth, and a hedge against terrestrial destruction. The two world wars, the great famines in the communist world, the rise of unsustainable consumerism and pollution, and especially the Cold War and the threat of nuclear annihilation made the earth's surface seem too dangerous a place to sustain human life. Biologists and physicians were even warning about future pandemics. With the outlook for planet earth so bleak, and outer space much too far away (and cold, dark, and empty at that) Evans was sure his idea would inspire others.

And it did. But not in the usual way that such projects evolve, or even originate. Though Evans had progressive instincts to begin with, he was actually acting on a revelation that came to him in his sleep. They weren't exactly dreams. They were more detailed, persistent, and eventually all-consuming. But the most remarkable thing about his 'visions', as he called them, was that they were shared by others. An international group of seemingly random people, having no knowledge of one another, experienced identical visions while sleeping. For each of them, it ended with the image of a red disk, surrounded by a black ring, and another outer ring, also red. And on waking, they had been compelled to find colored markers – or even crayons in one instance – and illustrate that simple design on a piece of paper, and then send it to Evans, whom none of them had ever met, and had no good reason to correspond with. They couldn't have known, but this same red and black icon had appeared in Evans' own dream of a world within the clouds. On receiving a dozen of these letters, all within the same week, each explaining the same "dreams" and including illustrations of the same red and black symbol, he knew that he was somehow part of a work-team gathered by a higher force he didn't understand. He immediately used his connections to arrange for all his twelve correspondents to fly to Dublin.

Some journalists caught wind of Evans' planned gathering, and he gave a brief interview playing up the scientific and utopian aspects of the project, but saying nothing about its origin in a vision, or how his team of collaborators had come together. The reporters began writing about his projects under headlines like "Are We Close to Living in the Clouds?". "Finally, The Promise of Heaven on Earth (or at Least Just Above it)!", "Hope for a New Era!", etc. An American journalist did not like Evans' formulation "The In-Between" so replaced it with "The World of Realms" which by the time of the Dublin gathering a few weeks later had become the de facto name.

Most of the self-selected group who attended Evan's closed conference were scientists and engineers like himself. But an elderly French woman stood out for being the only spiritual figure. She was known as "The Mother" in India, where she'd gone after WWII to live with an Indian guru, and had since organized her own ashram. Longer than the rest, she'd been receiving what she called "The Word". But only recently the visions compelled her to communicate with Evans, and thus learn that others had received them too. She'd recorded her visions in a journal, which she brought to Ireland, with meticulous drawings of how this world in the clouds should look, and even instructions for building it. There was a mixture of bewilderment and awe among the others when they flipped through the pages, as no one else's visions, despite being nearly identical in outline, had included so many details.

Their shared vision was of a series of transparent spheres, with crystals at their centers, containing communities of hundreds of people. Evans and his new collaborators spent hours studying and debating the meaning of it all, and of The Mother's journal. At the end of the one-week meeting, the conclusion was that the journal had indeed been inspired by whatever had brought them together. Most of them had trouble believing in a God or gods, so called it a "higher intelligence". That the team had come from all over the world with a signifying symbol to mark the authenticity of their visions was also taken as a sign that The World of Realms was meant to belong to everyone, maybe representing the next stage of human evolution. It would transcend the idea of nations and nationality, but would still exist as a series of separate communities, that would organically develop their own values and beliefs under some sort of supernatural guidance.

But one question loomed. The drawings in the Frenchwoman's journal looked too much like architecture designed for planet earth. There was no way such structures could stand on their own in mid-air, they thought. Their visions had not revealed how such communities were to float in the atmosphere. Was there a way? The team began to wonder if The Word had not been fully revealed to them. Perhaps more visions would naturally follow, now that they had congregated as a team. On returning home, they each willed themselves to sleep for many days hoping to see farther. But no one saw anything. Not even The Mother. "This is a test of faith," she said in a long-distance call to Evans one morning. The Mother believed it was their task to carry out the construction work on the ground, and the rest would be taken care of by whatever had brought them together.

But Evans did not buy into her reasoning. To him they were being challenged to use the best earthly science and technology to complete the vision, and lift the spheres into the air themselves. A debate ensued, and he eventually declared that those who wished to forge on without additional divine help, using only science, could stay, while the rest were free to leave. Only The Mother left. Before cutting ties, though, she warned of possible danger for going against The Word; of attempting to rely on science alone while ignoring the fact that a spiritual force had brought them together in the first place.

Evans and his colleagues knew nothing of what was happening in China at the same time. They sometimes wondered aloud if anyone in the communist world had also received visions. But even if they had, there was no possibility to communicate across the hard boundary of the Cold War, especially with a China then in the midst of Cultural Revolution. The publicity about the project in the West had eventually reached Nie, however, helping to confirm in his mind that his own visions must be real. Ironically, the details of Nie's visions were much closer to those of The Mother. Organville was in some sense the fulfilment of her more spiritual interpretation of The Word. But all that remained unknown to Evans until many, many years later - long after his own project had run its course. By that time The Mother was dead, and Evans could only reflect on how peculiar she would have found it that her "spiritual", faith-based plan eventually found fulfillment in a society that had utterly rejected religion as so much superstition.

Evans' wife Marianne was just finishing her entry for the fanciful "What does Your Realm Look Like?" contest sponsored by a Dublin newspaper when Evans swooped in and snatched the form away from her.

"My Realm will be one where people are honest with one another, where . . ." recited Evans halfway and raised the paper so that Marianne would not snatch it back.

"Give it back to me, you rat!" She pretended to be angry.

"So, love, tell me. What do you want your Realm to be like?" asked Evans as he lovingly handed the entry back to Marianne.

"Promise you will not laugh?" She gave a sheepish smile.

"Promise." Evans placed his right hand on his chest where the heart lay.

Marianne straightened her skirt, cleared her throat, and began painting a world where everyone was as transparent as the glass spheres they lived in. The complexities of the human psyche that theorists like Freud and Jung had posited would disappear. No subconscious mind to control and confuse behaviors, statements, or judgements. In other words, no one in Marianne's Realm would have a shadow self, only a "true" one, incapable of wearing masks. Humans would become more predictable in each other's eyes, and not surprise and hurt one another by sudden changes in personality, cryptic statements, and unexpected insults that came from dark recesses that opened and closed suddenly and without warning. It would be a world where everyone would have no reason not to trust one another. Everyone would speak their mind, but no one would feel pain, because honesty would be all they knew. Pain, to Marianne, came from confusion and distrust. There would be none of that in her Realm. Throughout, Marianne spoke like an excited child.

Evans listened intently, but then broke out in dark laughter. Marianne gave him an angry look for breaking his promise.

"Your world could not possibly exist, because we're not angels, but animals. We evolved from reptiles, with monkeys our close cousins. These layers of evolution are our legacy – the reason we have power struggles, tell lies, and harm each other, often without meaning to. You, Marianne, are the least aggressive and most honest person I've ever met. And the most fragile because of it. And when I try and see the world through your eyes, I hate it for disappointing you, even harming you with its hypocrisy. I can't change human nature. No one can. But perhaps, at least, I can give us both a fresh start in the clouds," he explained.

"But there must be others like me, sensitive enough to never try and hurt anybody. We could make a better world together."

"But if everyone were transparent, would it not be a world of hurt. Even our lies are often out of sensitivity, to save others' feelings, not wound them," retorted Evans.

"Everyone is already so glass-like. I mean in our fragility. But we're clouded glass, colored glass, to keep us from seeing into each other's souls. Add transparency to our glass-like selves, and we'd end up as broken shards," he continued.

"Not in my Realm," said Marianne.

"We're broken shards now. At least I am. I don't understand how you and others absorb all the insincerity, wear all your masks, change your opinions and facial expressions and even your voices depending on who you're talking to. Maybe you do it to survive. But I can't survive this way. And what you claim to value most – sincerity, honesty, speaking your mind without fear – none of that is true in practice. Science is supposed to be a search for the truth, isn't it? Where is the truth in even a cocktail party?"

"It's not just hypocrisy Marianne," said Evans.

"It's more diplomacy. Everyone is fragile. Everyone can be easily hurt. So we learn to be polite, mask our feelings, not say what we mean, or say it carefully, because of the reactions of others to our criticisms, or slip-ups. Social relations are a kind of dance in which we're trying hard not to step on other's toes. Because it hurts them, and they might be inclined to hurt us in return. We're all lumbering awkwardly around this dance-hall, crashing into one another and not keeping very good time to the music."

Marianne had revealed her ideal to Evans, who'd done nothing but criticize it as unrealistic, and in its own way, harmful. She crushed the paper and thrashed it on the floor before stomping out of their room as she always did when provoked. Alone, Evans picked up the crushed paper and neatened out the creases. For the rest of the day, he studied Marianne's masterplan. Could he actually make it happen? Create not just a utopia, but one tailored for her? He felt compelled to try. And despite what he'd said to her, he knew that her ideal Realm was close to his own.

In thinking about execution, Evans and his team came upon Buckminster Fuller's theory for Cloud 9, a huge geodesic sphere a mile wide which could rise into the atmosphere and stay there through a simple principle of physics. One peculiarity of a geodesic sphere is that the larger the construction, the stronger it becomes.

And the larger it is, the more air it naturally contains. It can even become buoyant – airborne - provided the air inside is heated. It's the same principle as a hot air balloon. But with a geodesic sphere of great size, just a degree or two higher than the outside temperature would do the trick. The dome could also contain people, according to Fuller. His dome was large, strong, and buoyant enough to theoretically float a community of 5,000 above the clouds. But it was all theory up till now. Not even a prototype had ever been built.

That would now change. After months of brainstorming, the team came up with a design for a Realm as a geodesic sphere, though only half the size of Fuller's. The outer shell would be made from the toughest glass, fully transparent, but also virtually crack-proof. In the middle would be a disc-shaped platform landscaped with gardens, fields, forests, ponds, and wetlands, with tree and plant species from all over the temperate part of the world. Future realms would have desert climates, tropical jungles, arctic landscapes, et cetera. But this first one would preserve the fauna of the middle of the northern hemisphere, where it was built. No animals inhabited this green oasis other than birds, bees, earthworms, and a few other insects and small creatures beneficial to the plants. Within this verdant landscape would live a few hundred humans, though they were expected to reproduce and thus expand their numbers in time. But modestly. These inhabitants would have to survive on what they grew or collected from their garden world. It would be a second Earth, completely self-sustained. There would be no returning to the other one.

Evans' family had extensive land holdings in the lightly-populated part of Wales called Snowdonia, just across the Irish Sea from Dublin. In one of these Welsh valleys, out of sight of governments and journalists, Evans' team built their geodesic spherical realm. It was a decade-long project, fully financed by Evan's own fortune, and protected by the fiction that it was an experimental device for deep-sea mining. Tests had shown that, true to Fuller's theory, the sphere could rise and be kept aloft simply using the power of the sun.

The largest problem to be overcome wasn't engineering, it turned out, but biological. Radiation reached such levels in the upper atmosphere, that no human could survive a whole lifetime there without getting radiation poisoning. Being a geneticist, Evans thought the solution lay in gene therapy, finding and 'switching on' genes that could improve human resistance to radiation. It was this research that would eventually result in his anti-aging discoveries, and the Xter pill. But back then, his one compelling thought was to give Marianne a chance at a second life in a better place. For he knew that his wife was too sensitive for the earthly world.

Once she'd learned of his project, Marianne's whole being was focused on escaping into the clouds in the new world her husband was creating. And her obsession with the Realm only grew with time. In a strange way it also compelled him forward. He knew that in perfecting the Realm, he was creating a world for the person he loved above all others. So it had better be as safe and perfect as he could make it.

Evans eventually developed a gene therapy that would allow human bodies to better withstand long-term exposure to low-dose radiation. But at great personal sacrifice. Like many medical researchers before him, he conducted the very first experiments on himself. By the time he'd found the key to protecting the others destined to live aloft, his own body had begun to weaken and deteriorate from too many injections. Of all the members of the team, and their families, and others they had carefully chosen to live in the colony above the clouds, only Evans was, in the end, too physically unfit to go. The only outward sign of his deterioration was peeling skin, but he knew that living at 30,000 feet would make him succumb to radiation sickness in a matter of weeks. He didn't tell this to Marianne, however. He let her think he'd accompany her, and when the day came for sphere to lift out of the valley, pulled by the power of the sun and the principle of convection, and with nearly 500 people ascending with it, he stepped off without warning at the very last moment. No one saw him do it, not even Marianne. And he didn't look back.

13 LOVE IN AN ONLINE BUBBLE

With the help of Chief Librarian Li, Li-An found the whereabouts of Professor Wu Dahai. Wu, now ninety-years old, was living alone in an old apartment in Guangzhou, where he was born. After the death of Chairman Mao, Wu was reinstated at the Genetics Department of Beijing University and worked there till retirement. He never published any papers on Organville, which with the death of Chairman Mao fell into oblivion. Wu neither engaged in active research nor attended conferences, so no one in the field remembered him in his old age. "Fate," uttered Chief Librarian Li after Li-An explained to him at length why she needed to see Wu. In the year she'd spent in Hong'an, the Chief Librarian and Li-An had become close. "I wouldn't disturb old Wu for anyone except you," said the Chief Librarian. The next day, Li-An received a call from him telling her he'd contacted Wu, and the old man was willing to see her.

After she bought the air tickets to Guangzhou, Li-An messaged White saying she'd like to meet him there. She didn't tell him that she was after his DNA sample. "I'll try my best," he wrote back. But after that, Li-An stopped receiving replies whenever she'd send White a text. She could still see his public postings, most of which were the usual company advertisements. Only occasionally would White post something personal. "He's back to work," thought Li-An to herself. One day she saw that White had posted a short video of himself, just lasting a few seconds. "Oh, I've been secretly video-ed," he'd written on top of the posting. It showed him walking towards the lift of what looked like the lobby of an office building. He looked formal, wearing suit and necktie, and draped in a matching winter outer coat. So, White was back to work and probably too busy to message. But not replying at all was extreme, Li-An kept thinking to herself. Why the sudden change? Had White lost interest in her? Did he prefer to just keep her as a distant friend on LetsChat and not meet? But that would be too bizarre, she told herself. The night before she was scheduled to fly, Li-An sent White one more text message. Still, no answer.

Li-An arrived in China early next morning. She'd chosen not to fly direct to Guangzhou but to stop first in Hong Kong. Li-An was buying herself a tall green tea latte at the Starbucks airport café before heading into the city when her phone buzzed. A white strip appeared on her cellphone screen. On the left was White's name in Chinese characters and underneath was his message, though only a small part was captured. Li-An slid her right index finger across to unlock the phone, then went into LetsChat to read his message.

17th February 2017, 9.48 am

"Li-An, I didn't contact you all this while because I didn't know what to say. I've been quiet also because I don't want you to be sad. I told you I'd try my best to meet you in Guangzhou, but was worried I might not make it. And my worries were right. I really can't find the time, so can't go. I know you really want us to meet and I believe you have imagined all kinds of scenarios. Me too. Li-An, the things I said to you, the way I looked at you, they were all real. I never meant to lie to you. But I really can't make it this time. I work in Beijing and Hebei, and I commute between these two places. Once a week, with only one day's rest in between (but only if we're not busy. Otherwise we don't rest at all). I can't exhaust myself. I also cannot apply for leave. I've been trying to find a way. I really wish I could tell you that, yes, I can make it to see you in Guangzhou. But in the end, I can't. I'm so sorry. I can't find a way. I've disappointed you, Li-An. I'm sorry again. I will miss you."

17th February 2017, 10.32 am

"I hope we can still be like before . . .
"

17th February 2017, 11.06 am

"Thank you for your text message," was Li-An's reply half an hour later, unable to get a grip on her feelings, but relieved that he'd at least replied.

"My wish is for you to be happy every day. I like to see you smile," wrote White.

The next day, Li-An took the train to Guangzhou where she'd booked two nights at Fraser Suites. It was the same hotel chain she'd used in Tianjin, but this building was older. Li-An knew that because she'd stayed in the hotel a few years earlier, in the summer of 2013. The campus apartment Grey had reserved for her had been too hot, really unbearable. The mosquitoes were small enough to penetrate the netting, and kept her awake the entire night. Finding herself absolutely sleep-deprived and her limbs scarred from mosquito bites, she'd decided to move to the city, and found Fraser Suites Guangzhou. "Shipaiqiao subway station?" Grey had asked again for confirmation. Li-An nodded her head. Out of politeness, she'd made sure to inform him that she was temporarily abandoning the quarters he'd found for her. "Yes, there are a few youth hostels in that area," he said. Li-An nodded, not bothering to explain that she was actually checking into a forty-nine square meter studio executive with a king-sized bed, living room and kitchenette.

So Li-An booked the same hotel again this trip. But this time it was mostly for White. She was hoping that in the end he'd come and find her, but was mostly just grateful that they were back in touch. As soon as she checked into the room, Li-An took out the two cheongsams she'd bought in a shop in Hong Kong and photographed them with her cellphone. Ever since White had stopped communicating with her, Li-An would spend hours listening to the soundtrack of Wong Kar Wai's *In the Mood for Love*. She was particularly drawn to the number *Yumeji's Theme* for its sad wistful melody. One night, as if on a whim, Li-An googled and found the tailor who'd outfitted the lead actress: Linva tailor. 38 Cochrane Street, Hong Kong.

18th February 2017, 4.36 pm

"My new qipao. Which do you like better?" asked Li-An after she'd sent White the cheongsam photos. She knew he was more familiar with qipao, which was the actual Chinese expression, while cheongsam was transliterated from Cantonese.

18th February 2017, 4.53 pm

"The second one," replied White, who also added a smiley winking one eye with tongue sticking out. The one in the second picture was undoubtedly sexier, being made of silk.

18th February 2017, 5.20 pm

"Here, check my room out." Li-An then sent White photos of the hotel room as if by doing so, he could still have a presence there.

The next day after a late breakfast, Li-An decided to go shopping. She headed for the most luxurious mall in town, Taikoo Hui, located just opposite her hotel. But she found the price tags too expensive. Even Giordano, which Li-An knew was not marketed as a high luxury brand outside of China, sold a woman's top at a staggering 2000 yuan! 400 Kramen dollars. Li-An immediately walked out of the store and towards the underground connection between the mall and Shipaiqiao subway station. Exit C. She headed for the opposite end, turned left for Exit A where an escalator took her to the basement of OneLink Walk which adjoined Fraser Suites. Hotwind Classics. The first store Li-An saw on her right as she stepped into the mall. A shoe shop. There was a crowd and Li-An knew a sale was going on. "Maybe it's time to get myself a couple pair of shoes," she thought to herself and made her way into the shop. "Ah, this should go nicely with my silk cheongsam." Li-An tried on a pair of grey velvety high-heels with strings tied in a ribbon at the back. She asked for a new pair but there weren't any in stock. Li-An decided to get the one on display. She then tried on a classic court shoe in shiny black. There was a new pair in stock for this design. Li-An proceeded to the cashier and took out a wad of Chinese yuan from her wallet. Unlike the locals, Li-An could not settle the bill through LetsPay. She never stayed in China long enough to have a permanent phone number, which was required to activate the pay system on LetsChat. Li-An could pay using the "red packet money" she'd received from friends and most recently White, but they were not enough for the shoes, so she ended up paying cash.

Next, Li-An took the escalator up to Level One and saw ZARA Home. She caught sight of the lingerie section located just by the entrance, smiled surreptitiously, and stepped into the shop. Li-An scanned the displays and picked out two nightdresses. After making sure that they were the right size and in perfect condition, she went straight to the cashier. There was no time to try them on. She had an appointment at two-thirty. Back in her room, Li-An hung the two pajamas in the closet. Then came an idea. She took one down and placed it on the bed behind her. With her cellphone, Li-An took a picture of the one that was still hanging in the closet. Next, she took that one down, hung the other one up, and again took a snapshot. She then posted the two pictures to White.

19th February 2017, 1.41 pm

"Which one do you like?" asked Li-An

"The first one." replied White almost immediately. He'd also added the same smiley with tongue sticking out. The one he preferred was the sexier of the two. White lucent satin with lace covering the front., exposing the breasts.

"This is so fun," wrote Li-An.

"What are you doing?" asked White.

"I just got back from shopping."

"Sexy lingerie..." teased Li-An.

"You knew I'd like that piece better." White added a smiley with finger pointing at Li-An.

"The second piece is for me to wear on regular days. The sexier one is for you." Li-An was pleased at how White managed to bring out her cheeky side.

"You are naughty," quipped White.

"Come to Beijing," he added.

19th February 2017, 1.50 pm

"I will take good care of myself so that when we finally meet, I'll give you my all," wrote Li-An lovingly.

White replied fifteen minutes later with two hugs. By this time, she was already in a cab on her way to meet Professor Wu, but smiled contentedly at his posting. As far as Li-An was concerned, this had already turned out to be a fruitful trip. Not only were they back in touch, he'd become more loving towards her. Their "chemistry" must match. It had to.

"Tell me, why are you here?" Despite his age, Wu's voice was not feeble but firm and confident. Li-An thought he looked at most in his sixties, though this was impossible.

"It was Professor Evans who told me to find you." Li-An reminded herself to be careful, and not disclose anything about Evans' medical trials.

"Yes, that *laowai*. Soon after the Chairman died, he came to China and we met," recalled Wu. Laowai, literally "old foreigner".

"You are not what you seem, he said. Something was done to you, is that right?"

Li-An was shocked. Except Evans and his research team, nobody could tell Li-An had undergone an anti-aging process. How did Wu know? She nodded her head nevertheless.

"But why come to me when you're already like this." He surveyed her from top to toe.

"I'm grateful for the good looks, but wish it had come the natural way. Professor Evans told me you might be able to help." Li-An gave Wu a furtive look, hoping she'd not said anything offensive. And indeed, for a long time Wu did not answer her.

"The natural way?" Wu broke out in laughter while Li-An blushed. He was right. According to the law of nature, humans grow older and less attractive with age, not the opposite.

"Do you see anything unusual about me?" Wu finally broke his silence.

"You're also more youthful-looking than you should be," answered Li-An matter-of-factly.

"And it's not necessarily a good thing. I look around me. All my friends are gone. My wife too, everyone except me. I've already lived a lifetime. I've had enough. God knows how long more I have to stay on this planet," Wu looked wistful as he spoke.

"This must be a result of your time in Organville, no?" asked Li-An. Wu nodded his head as he lit a cigarette.

"I heard from Old Li that you wrote a dissertation about my work there." Wu took a draw of the cigarette and slowly walked out of his apartment. He beckoned Li-An to follow suit. They walked down two flight of stairs to an open patio in front of the building. Wu slumped into one of the rattan armchairs, crossed his legs, and looked up. Li-An sat opposite him, keeping silent till he was ready to speak again.

"They are all up there," Wu pointed his right index finger at the sky. Li-An knew he was referring to the "Great China World of Realm".

"You mean it all came true?" Li-An asked in disbelief.

"Yes, it worked. We followed the plan and it worked," Wu turned to look in her eyes. Li-An had never dared to imagine that scenario he was so matter-of-factly describing. So, this was what Evans meant by "the full story".

"But nobody can prove that it exists up there, no?" she asked.

"It was not simply an architectural marvel," Wu spoke to himself aloud, ignoring Li-An.

"The building strictly followed the instructions laid out in the plan; the one that came to Comrade Nie in a series of visions, which he recorded and shared with me," he continued.

"And the surgical operation done on every single individual. It sounded insane, but it was also in the plan, so we carried it out, and everyone survived. Only then could the aura or magnetic field be harnessed. Evans called it an energy field. Quantum physics calls it particles. It's the same, just a different way of putting it," explained Wu.

"The crystal ball inside the sphere trapped and absorbed the particles of the upper atmosphere. It was the source of all the transformations that took place in the village. The villagers began living in harmony, creating an aura of blissfulness which fed back to the crystal. A magnetic field began surrounding the village, and growing in strength with each passing day. Finally, the day came when its strength reached beyond 2000 T. Both Comrade Nie and I saw the needle on the compass moving frantically before it finally broke. Luckily, Comrade Nie had commissioned a physicist to invent a magnetometer to pick up supra-normal frequencies."

"That was the night when the bright glow emanated from the village, wasn't it?" Li-An followed up.

"When it started, everyone entered the sphere. Except me. Before my eyes, the physical structure and all the people in it just disappeared, but the magnetic field remained. It is probably still there, though weaker. If you find the actual spot where the crystal was, you may still be able to detect the energy field. I told that to Evans. That must be why he sent you." Wu turned to look at Li-An in the eyes.

"Where exactly is it? Which part of Beijing?" Li-An asked excitedly.

"Sanlitun, Chaoyang District," said Wu.

"But where exactly?" Li-An sounded impatient.

"I can't tell you. It was too long ago and too much has changed. You'll only know once you enter into the field, if you can find it." replied Wu.

"And what will happen if I'm in it?" Li-An looked intently at Wu for the answer.

"I don't know." Wu looked into the sky and pondered for a while.

"But Professor Evans told me you might be able to help . . ." Li-An tried to break the silence but ended up being interrupted by Wu.

"Look, it's been a long time. Everything I wanted to say is in those boxes. And the voice recordings. I don't know any more. And I don't know what will happen once you find and step into the field. All I know is the place is now a prime location in Beijing, and is said to have the best *fengshui*. That can't be a coincidence." Wu said matter-of-factly.

"I don't even know if they're alive." He stubbed out the cigarette – his third one – against the ashtray sitting on his lap, and got up to signal that the conversation was over.

"Why didn't you go with them?" Li-An's question made Wu pause for a moment, but he shook his head, either to indicate he didn't know, or it wasn't her place to ask.

Without bidding Li-An goodbye, Wu began climbing the stairs back to his apartment.

The next day at noon, Li-An checked out of Fraser Suites and took the subway to another hotel, where she'd stay for three more nights before returning to Kramen Island. Guangdong Victory Hotel was located on an island in Guangzhou city, called Shamian. Arriving there, Li-An felt as though she'd crossed back in time. The island, untouched by China's fast-paced industrialization, retained the old architecture from the colonial period, when the city was called Canton. Guangdong Victory Hotel had two separate wings, East and West. Li-An's room, which came with a balcony, was in the West wing. This was the more historic part of the building, and Li-An was glad she'd made that choice. Sitting alone in the balcony, Li-An admired the columns and other architectural features. She sat there for a long time before returning to the room to find her phone.

"I'm here in Guangzhou," wrote Li-An to Grey, who'd by now descended way down in her LetsChat messaging board.

"How many more days will you be here?" Grey wrote back minutes later.

"Two" was her short reply.

Within a half hour Grey replied: "I just got air tickets. I'll be touching down at noon tomorrow. I'll call you when I get to the hotel."

It was the evening. Li-An sent White three pictures of her new hotel room. One had the view of the bed, while another was of the bathroom. Li-An's photo caught her own reflection in the bathroom mirror placed above the bathtub adjacent to the wash basin. The bathroom was an open concept, separated from the bedroom by a sliding door fitted right behind the wash basin. An unusual design, Li-An thought to herself. The last picture was of the balcony showing a chair and part of the table against the night sky.

20th February 2017, 7.15 pm
"I changed to another hotel. In old Guangzhou. Shamian Island," Li-An informed White after she'd sent the pictures over.

20th February 2017, 7.17 pm

"Take good care of yourself," wrote White, who also added two hug icons.

"You too," replied Li-An.

White's prompt reply excited Li-An. These days, she never knew when or if White would reply.

"Take your meals promptly," he added.

"And drink more water." Li-An was reminded of his messages to her the morning they arrived at Tianjin last December.

"I will," she replied.

20th February 2017, 7.20 pm

"What is your next plan?" White asked.

"I don't know," wrote Li-An truthfully.

"Xiao Yang (You little mischief)," teased White, who obviously had no idea what Li-An was thinking or going through.

"I'll phrase it another way. What do you want in life?" wrote White.

"Work, love, qipao, a place where I can flourish. Most importantly, a place where I can feel alive," explained Li-An.

"You don't have high expectations, do you?"

"I just want to go with my feelings." But Li-An knew deep down she couldn't. Still, she enjoyed creating an image of free-spiritedness.

"I'll add one more condition."

"What is it?"

"No lack of food." White added a smiley with hand covering mouth. Eyes were an inverted U to express cheeky embarrassment.

"Yes, that's a basic but important requirement," Li-An wrote back.

"And one more."

"No lack of money to spend," White declared.

"Yes, that too." She was beginning to wonder why he kept harping on practical things.

"Talk about your family." White followed up with yet another practical question.

"I don't know. I can't talk about them," she responded.

For a long time, Li-An waited but White did not reply. She soon fell asleep.

Li-An's first day with Grey

21ˢᵗ February 2017, 1.05 pm

"My flight was delayed. I just touched down," wrote Grey.
"I'll call you once I reach the hotel," he added.
While waiting for Grey to arrive, Li-An took a stroll around Shamian island. As she stood on the street facing her balcony window, Li-An took out her cellphone and snapped a shot. She continued down the road, turned the corner to the left and saw a Starbucks. Li-An went in, got herself a tall hojicha latte, and found a seat in the open balcony area.

21ˢᵗ February 2017, 1.42 pm

"Shamian island is very romantic. This is the view of my balcony." Li-An searched for the photo of her room balcony and posted it to White.

21ˢᵗ February 2017, 2.00 pm

"Good. I'm glad you're staying somewhere comfortable," replied White. This time, it took him about 20 minutes to reply.

21ˢᵗ February 2017, 2.18 pm

"It's older, but it has more character than the previous hotel," reported Li-An.
Just then, Li-An received a voice call from Grey. She pressed the green icon, and placed the phone to her ear. "I'm here at the hotel," he said. Li-An left Starbucks and walked towards her hotel, which was only five minutes away. But she didn't see Grey. Li-An picked up the phone and called him. "Where are you?" she asked. "I'm standing at the lobby," he answered. "You must be in the East Building. I'm here in the West wing. Stay there. I'll come get you." Li-An hung up and exited the hotel. She turned right, walked straight along the side street where she'd earlier taken the photo of her room balcony, then turned right again and walked even further

down along the main street before reaching the East Building. Upon entering the building, Li-An immediately sighted Grey. "Come, follow me." As they headed for the other wing, neither of them spoke.

Arriving at the front desk, Grey presented his ID to the receptionist who recorded his details and issued him another card key. Li-An and Grey then took the lift up to their hotel room. "This is pretty neat," commented Grey on the room upon entering. "High ceiling. Typical of 19th century architecture. There's even an old computer. Have you tried using it?" Li-An shook her head. She suddenly felt uneasy with Grey being in the same room with her, as though he was a complete stranger. "Let's take a seat at the balcony. First, let me boil some water," said Grey, who had a habit of packing sachets of tea leaves in his backpack whenever he traveled. Li-An went first to sit in the balcony. Ten minutes later, Grey emerged with a cup of tea in one hand and sat on the chair across the table from Li-An, who then stood up and went to lean against the balcony. "What does *xiao yang* mean?" Li-An looked out of the balcony as she spoke. "It's a Northern Chinese slang. It's used to tease the opposite sex, but especially females," he explained. "How about one having a kind of scent?" Li-An was trying to clarify the Chinese phrase *you wei dao*, which White had used on her. "It usually means someone is alluring." "And *qi zhi*?" "That one carries himself or herself well." "Oh, I see," replied Li-An, who made her way back into the room and sat on one side of the bed. Grey soon came and sat next to Li-An, who slightly turned her head away from him. Grey gently wrapped his arm around her shoulders. But Li-An looked away even more. In her head, she kept repeating White's name. "Li-An, how have you been? I miss you," Grey started caressing her back. Li-An quickly stood up, walked a few steps away from him, then turned to face Grey again. She leaned against the sliding door that separated the room from the balcony. "I'm fine," Li-An looked furtively at the carpeted floor as she spoke.

Li-An's second day with Grey

22nd February 2017, 4.52 pm

"I had the hairstylist cut a fringe out. Does it look good?" As Grey was taking a nap, Li-An quietly took a snapshot of herself in front of the half-length mirror that stretched the entire length of the bathtub.

The picture showed Li-An sporting a side fringe combed to the left. She was framed by the flower prints bordering the mirror. Li-An did not look straight into the mirror but down at the cellphone.

22nd February 2017, 5.06 pm

"Not bad at all," was White's reply.
"You carry yourself well. You look good regardless," he added.

22nd February 2017, 5.11 pm

"If I come to Beijing, will you find me?" Li-An checked and saw that Grey was still snoozing away on the bed.

22nd February 2017, 5.22 pm

"Lai ba". "Come," was White's reply.

22nd February 2017, 5.29 pm

"Then I'll make plans to go to Beijing." Li-An followed her message with the regular smiley face.
"Always keep that smile," wrote White.
Grey woke up from his nap. "Good timing," Li-An thought to herself and put her phone away.

The third day

23rd February 2017, 10.12 am

"Good morning, I'm about to board the plane for Kramen Island." She'd just parted with Grey, who'd gone to the domestic flight section of Baiyun International Airport. Alone by herself and waiting at the gate for boarding, Li-An thought about White and wrote him a message.

"Have a safe journey. I miss you, Li-An," replied White.

"I'll come find you in Beijing. In return, you must keep me company every night." (Smiley with eyes in inverted U, but mouth grinning in broad U-shape. Cheeks colored with two strips of pink.)

"You are so naughty."

"I'm boarding. Goodbye."

"Goodbye, Li-An."

23ʳᵈ February 2017, 6.39 pm

"I'm home. I'm all showered and lying in bed," wrote Li-An to White. Her plane touched down Kramen Island an hour ago, and she was eager to return home, shower, and write to White.

"Rest well tonight," White replied.

"Thank you for keeping me company the past couple days. There're things I want to tell you. You don't have to reply me. Just read."

"Thank you, Li-An," White wrote back immediately.

23ʳᵈ February 2017, 6.41 pm

"I'm in love, but with a stranger. It's so unbelievable and yet so magical," wrote Li-An.

"I can only think about the present moment. I don't dare think about the future," She continued.

23ʳᵈ February 2017, 6.48 pm

"You can," wrote White.

"I really enjoyed my time with you on LetsChat the past couple weeks." Li-An saw White's reply but chose to ignore it. After all, he didn't know the context to which he was replying.

"I don't know what you mean by "just like before"." White had written it the morning Li-An arrived in Hong Kong.

23ʳᵈ February 2017, 7.19 pm

"All I know is I love you. I don't know you very well but at this moment, my feelings for you are very strong." Li-An started tearing up as she wrote.

"I can only go with my feelings. The rest I don't know. So I can't go back to before."

Li-An didn't wish to return to the time before their first videochat, if that was what White meant. She wanted something to happen between them. Something romantic. She couldn't bring herself to be more explicit, but hoped deep down he knew what she was alluding to.

14. A BEIJING PROMISE

28th February 2017, 6.40 pm

"I'm all showered, and am now lying in bed, reading. I want to show you pictures of my apartment. It's rented." Li-An mentioned her lack of property ownership to create the impression that she was not only younger than White, but of the same financial and social standing. She assumed he didn't have much at this point.

28th February 2017, 6.40 pm

"My bedroom, the living room and kitchen, and a bathroom." Li-An had taken the pictures soon after getting out of the shower. Hers was a small, squarish studio.

"Ni ne." "And you?" White's reply excited her. Li-An knew from past experience that it was the time of the day he would still be busy.

"You should be in the photos too."

Li-An immediately took a selfie lying on her stomach in bed, her chin propped against her left hand. Her wet hair was wrapped in a well-worn greyish towel tied in a knot at the tip of her head. The picture revealed half her breasts.

"You are forever so sexy," responded White.

"De se," he teased Li-An. (northern slang for "show off".)

"All the better for you," Li-An remarked cheekily.

"You are naughty as always." White then added a laughing smiley with tongue sticking out and V-shaped eyes with the tip pointing towards each other in the middle.

"Ni zai zuo sha." "What are you doing?" asked Li-An. Sha: the mainland Chinese slang for "what". Li-An was getting accustomed to using such slang in her conversations with White.

"I'm heading out to eat dinner," replied White, who then sent a ten-second video of him walking towards the lift in an office lobby. It was the same clip he'd posted weeks ago, the one his colleague had taken without him knowing.

28th February 2017, 6.45 pm

"Someone secretly took it while I was at work," White explained.
"I know," acknowledged Li-An.

28th February 2017, 6.48 pm

"It's your female admirer. It has to be," Li-An felt jealous as she wrote.
"She's my colleague," corrected White.
"A colleague that admires you." Li-An felt uneasy despite herself.
"There are six of us in my team, three males and three females. The three girls like to secretly take pictures of me." White added the smiley with hand over mouth, eyes an inverted U. Li-An wasn't sure if White was genuinely embarrassed or was flattered deep down, but tried his best not to show it.
"They like to do this for fun."
"Xiang ni la." "I miss you," Li-An wrote purposefully.
"Let's video chat tonight," White wrote back. For a second, Li-An couldn't believe he'd made the offer.
"I miss you too," wrote White again.
"What time?" asked Li-An excitedly.
"9 pm."
"9 pm it is."
"See you later tonight," Li-An wrote her last message, then exited from LetsChat.

28th February 2019, 9.05 pm

"I'm ready." It was five minutes past nine. White had not called her, so Li-An decided to send him a text. Just then the phone sounded. Li-An quickly placed her phone on the two pillows stacked on top of each other against the bed frame. She neatened her pajama, then pressed the answer button.

"Ni hao. It's been a while," smiled Li-An shyly.

"Yes, indeed," replied White.

"She's not back from work yet? Your girlfriend?" Li-An suddenly recalled that White actually had a girlfriend.

"We don't live together," White replied matter-of-factly.

"What you're seeing is my dormitory. She works in another city," explained White, who noticed the curious look in Li-An's face.

"Oh I see," replied Li-An. Up to now she'd thought White was cohabiting with his girlfriend and communicating with her secretly. But it turned out his situation was just like most middle- class Chinese couples who worked in separate cities and only reunited during national holidays.

"It's warm in here. Give me a second. I need to remove my shirt." White took off his top to reveal a well-toned body. Li-An figured it was the heating system in his dormitory that made him feel warm. All buildings in northern China were installed with heaters, unlike in the south.

"Take off your clothes," ordered White. Like a robot obeying a command, Li-An stood up on her knees and slid the straps of her pajama down to her waist to reveal her breasts. It was the less sexy one she'd gotten at ZARA Home in her last trip to Guangzhou.

"I want everything removed." Again, Li-An did as she was told.

"Ni zhe ge xiao yao jing." You little demon. The term *yao jing* could also be used to describe an extremely attractive woman.

"You've totally beguiled me." White then reached his left hand for the lighted cigarette that until now had been beyond Li-An's view. White took a quick draw, blew out a puff of smoke, and placed the cigarette back in its original place. All this while, Li-An was looking down in embarrassment, her right arm placed diagonally across her chest hoping it'd cover some of her breasts.

"Take off your panty too." Li-An obeyed and acted out his command.

"Let me see you down there."

"Bu yao!" "No!" Li-An broke out in resistance, but her voice was still gentle and soft. Amused and charmed by her reaction, White let out a smile.

"Alright, I'll respect your wishes," White replied comfortingly.

"Big Brother, what are we now?" Li-An asked.

"Li-An, let me tell you this. You really are my type. But the problem is you don't know me, and I don't know you. I'll only know after we spend some time together," answered White, who went to take another puff of his cigarette.

"But do you like me?" probed Li-An. White nodded his head.

"See, I'm very busy during this period. But when you come, I'll take some time off. I can't promise anything, but I'll try my best." Li-An wasn't comfortable with his reply but tried her best not to show it.

"I'm curious. You have such fine qualities. Surely you must have many suitors, no?" But Li-An didn't answer White, her mind still disturbed by his non-committal response. Just then, they both heard a knock on White's door. He quickly placed his hand on the knob to prevent the person on the other side from opening it. White was clearly protecting Li-An, who was still naked, from being exposed to a third party.

"Li-An, I have to go. We'll talk again?" Li-An nodded in deference.

"Give Ge (big brother) a smile." Li-An smiled, directing her gaze downwards. When she looked up again, Li-An saw that White was smiling back. He was obviously pleased with her.

"Ok. You take care. I'll see you in Beijing." White's more reassuring tone this time put Li-An at ease.

3 days later

3rd March 2017, 9.50 pm

"Ge, you said in our last video chat you'd try your best to see me in Beijing. The reason I'm coming to Beijing is so that we can meet. There are important things I need to tell you," Li-An carefully typed out the last sentence but told herself to stop there.

3rd March 2017, 9.56 pm

"Li-An, I'll be in Beijing between 20th of March and 2nd of April. I was supposed to be in Hebei but my shift has been changed. You can come between those days. The problem is I'll be busy during this period. My company is launching a new development project. I'll try to take a day off, but honestly, I can't guarantee anything." Li-An's heart dropped, but she tried not to show it in her next reply.

3rd March 2017, 10 pm

"Fine. I'll let you know once I book the air-tickets," replied Li-An.

"Sure," White wrote back.

2 days later

6th March 2017, 7.05 pm

"Do I look good in qipao?" That evening, Li-An posted a picture of herself wearing the silky grey cheongsam she'd gotten in Hong Kong. She remembered White had preferred this to the purple checkered one.

"It's not just good. It's very good!" White replied instantly.

"You will be in Beijing 20th March to 2nd April, confirmed?" asked Li-An.

"Yes."

"Roger. When I come to Beijing, I want you to find me every night," Li-An wrote affectionately.

"To be honest, I can't promise every night. I'm worried things might crop up in the last minute. I hope for your understanding."

"But will you try your best?" pleaded Li-An.

"Of course."

"I don't know when we will have the chance to meet after this," Li-An cast a wistful glance at herself in the mirror facing her.

"Why do you say that?!" White added a red-colored, furious-looking icon.

"This thing called fate," Li-An wrote pessimistically.

Increasingly, Li-An was full of uncertainties about her plans, starting with meeting White to get his DNA sample. What if Evans rejected it in any case? And when she met White, should she tell him the truth about herself? She thought she couldn't bring herself to do that, and face his possible rejection. Or should she go to Beijing and finding the energy field at Sanlitun? But so what if she found it? Nobody, not even Professor Wu, knew what would happen. Li-An no longer knew which path to take.

2 days later

8ᵗʰ March 2017, 4.03 pm

"I just bought my air-tickets. I'll arrive in Beijing the afternoon of March 26ᵗʰ and return to Kramen Island on April 3ʳᵈ. I'll send you the hotel address the night before I come to Beijing," wrote Li-An chirpily.

Many hours passed and Li-An didn't hear from White. She was starting to wonder if he was displeased with something she'd posted earlier, the reference to fate.

8ᵗʰ March 2017, 7.01 pm

"Ge, I wrote on Monday that I might not see you after this and you posted an angry face. I was touched when I saw it. Thank you. There's something I want to confide in you. I've been in a dilemma the past couple days about whether or not I should come to Beijing. In the end, I bought the tickets. Look, I know very well the difference between reality and fantasy. I'm a perfectly normal person, just that we've been communicating on LetsChat. It's only real when we meet. I really wish to see you."

Li-An wrote openly about her feelings, hoping they would elicit a reply from White, who for days had not communicated with her. Still, she got no reply.

Many days passed

17ᵗʰ March 2017, 7.31 pm

"Ge, I've decided on the hotel to stay in Beijing. I'm going to send the pictures over now."

Li-An sent a picture of the room followed by a map showing the location of the hotel. She'd spent the entire afternoon searching for a suitable room on sleepeasy.com. Finally, Li-An decided on the Cendre Hotel. The photos on the website matched Li-An's taste. It was a boutique hotel decorated in Muji-esque style. The wooden flooring and furniture contrasted well with the whitewashed walls.

"I'd also like you to take me to 798 or watch Peking opera," wrote Li-An, referring to the famous 798 art district.

"If you're free, that is."

"But please don't ignore me," pleaded Li-An.

17th March 2017, 8.04 pm

"Did I hurt you with things I said previously? If I did, please tell me. Please don't clam up on me," Li-An wrote desperately half an hour later.

Still there was no reply from White. He'd just posted a public picture of the night sky in Beijing, so Li-An knew he wasn't dead or injured, but avoiding her on purpose.

Three nights later, Li-An woke suddenly from her sleep. She sat upright, her back leaning against the bed frame, and reached for the phone on the side table to her right. She clicked on LetsChat and began typing her thoughts on their message board. Tears were trickling down her face.

20th March 2017, 1.15 am

"Ge, I'm really exhausted. I don't want to keep guessing what's in your mind and I don't know why you're doing this to me. You told me to tell you all the happy and sad things in my life. But as soon as I shared how I felt, you started ignoring me. Why?" Li-An was determined to pour out her soul.

"I have a secret" she began to write, but then stopped herself and quickly deleted the message. She lay back in bed and cried herself to sleep.

The next morning, Li-An was woken by a 'click' sound. She knew White had finally replied to her. Li-An rolled over and picked up the phone. It was the first time in days that she'd seen White's headshot appear on her mobile screen.

20ᵗʰ March 2017, 9.55 am

"We are exceptionally busy during this period. I wake up at 5 in the morning, and go to bed past midnight. Too many things. All kinds. I hope you understand. I told you this before. This period I'm very busy, so you take good care of yourself. My liver is firing up. I'm now eating Chinese medicine. I'm also not getting enough sleep these days. I now have two huge eye bags. I can't catch up, my energy. But our mass training is over soon. Please don't worry. Take good care of yourself. This is more important than anything else. Understand? Be well."

Li-An didn't write White any more messages after that for fear they'd backfire. But she'd frequently check her LetsChat account for his postings. They were mainly sales posters, though one day, White posted a picture of himself standing in line with his colleagues, all of them wearing the same outfit. White shirt with classic blue jacket and pants. The next day, Li-An saw White had posted a second group photo. He and his colleagues stood around a massive model of a real estate development, the camera looking down on them. Li-An surveyed the few females that were in the picture.

25ᵗʰ March 2017, 10.29 pm

"I'll be using this number in Beijing tomorrow." Li-An sent a picture of the invoice of the phone number she'd bought while in Tianjin. She had a number of China sim cards that she used depending on the location to save on "foreign land" costs. A card purchased in the north would be charged higher if used in the south.
Again, no reply from White. Li-An was really getting desperate.

It was late afternoon when Li-An touched down at Beijing Capital International Airport. Upon clearing immigration, she headed straight to the basement taxi stand. There was nobody waiting in line. Li-An went to the first cab in queue. The driver didn't bother to get out from his seat to help with the luggage, but Li-An was accustomed to being treated this way in China.

The Cendre Hotel, situated behind the famous medicinal outlet Beijing Tongrentang, was a three-story boutique hotel. Its white façade was in stark contrast to the low, dark, and uniform residential blocks along the same alley. On entering, Li-An was greeted by two eager young employees behind the reception counter. "I have a reservation," she said while fishing for her passport and credit card. As she waited to be checked in, Li-An glanced around her. A dining area occupied half the lobby floor space. Framed portraits hung on the side of the wall facing the entrance. Li-An found the lobby lighting soothing. "Please follow me." The female employee ushered Li-An to a small flight of stairs in the back and up to her room, no. 108.

Li-An was impressed. The room was exactly the same as the pictures shown on the booking website, which was rare. The bricks of the wall were exposed but painted a slick white. Li-An took a quick look at the bathroom and saw a standalone bathtub on legs. But what struck her most was that the designer had done the entire bathroom – from the wall to the floor –in white square ceramic tiles with chipped edges so that smaller black ones may be fitted in each corner. The black tiles were inverted to look like diamonds. Li-An thought the bathroom had the same trippy feeling as Evans' laboratory. The rest of the room had wooden flooring. To her delight, Li-An saw that next to the bed was a walk-in dressing room. Inside she noticed a white-colored safe at the bottom left corner, its door half open. "That reminds me," thought Li-An to herself. She took out the passport from the purse slung on her right shoulder, placed it into the safe, and set the password to lock it. Back in Kramen Island, she'd imagined herself in the bathroom while White fiddled around with her things and found her passport, flipped to the identification page, saw her birthdate, and left her in shock and anger. She wasn't ready for White to find out her age. At least not that way.

That night, Li-An deliberated whether to contact White again, but in the end was afraid to try. Exhausted from the plane ride, she slowly drifted off to sleep. But when she woke up the next morning at 7.20 am, Li-An picked up her phone, plucked up all the courage she could gather, and dialed White's number. "Do, do..." the phone started ringing, followed by a voice "Wei." "Hello." Li-An recognized the voice. "Wei. Is this Bai Xiang?" She asked. "Oh, it's you Li-An." White sounded half-asleep. "Why are you using a Nanjing number?" he asked. She didn't answer White but started interrogating him. "Where are you?" "Hebei." White sounded awkward. "So it's all a lie? You knew all along you'd be in Hebei, but told me Beijing instead?" Li-An tried her best to sound calm, but it wasn't working. There was only silence on the other end. "Let me drink some water," said White, and slowly cleared his throat. "I can't come to Beijing," he finally answered. "Why didn't you tell me earlier?" Li-An kept pressing. "Ni zhe nü hai." "What a girl." Li-An thought she heard White chuckling and became really irritated. "Are you taking me for a fool? You told me to come but you're actually in Hebei!" The line was suddenly cut off. White had ended the call.

27th March 2017, 7.33 am

"It's not convenient for me to talk now," wrote White to Li-An on LetsChat.

"I'll call you."

"Don't reply to LetsChat."

"Couldn't you tell it was not convenient for me to talk just now?"

Li-An slowly got out of bed, washed her face, got dressed and headed to the lobby for breakfast. Even as she sipped her hot Earl Grey tea, she felt her body trembling inside. Why wasn't it convenient for White to talk just now? Was there a girl sleeping next to him? Was it one of his female colleagues? "What a girl" was White's remark over the phone just now, but what did it mean? Did it mean he was just fooling around with her?" With so many thoughts in her head, Li-An took a long time to finish breakfast. Back in the room, she decided to text White, despite being told not to.

27th March 2017, 9.57 am

"I told you right from the start not to play around with me. I'm such a fool. My heart is in so much pain," wrote Li-An while starting to weep.

"But I can't bring myself to delete you. You do it!" Li-An meant unfriending White on LetsChat.

She waited, but White did not call her. Neither did he remove her from LetsChat. That night, Li-An messaged Grey. "I'm in Beijing." Half an hour later, Grey replied. "How long will you be here?" he asked. "I return the afternoon of 3rd April", she answered. An hour later, Grey replied to say he'd come to Beijing to see her in a couple of days.

The next morning

28th March 2017, 7.13 am

"Please fulfill your promise to call me. I don't want to end like this," wrote Li-An to White the next morning.

28th March 2017, 7.57 am

"I'll call you soon," replied White.

One hour later, White called Li-An, who had been waiting by the phone the whole time. "Why didn't you tell me you're not in Beijing but Hebei?" Li-An was determined to get an answer. "I'll tell you, Li-An. I can't talk for too long. I'm at work. Listen, I was telling the truth. I was supposed to be in Beijing this period but the management changed my schedule," replied White. "I was angry too. I had plans to bring you sightseeing in Beijing. But I have my rice bowl to take care of. If I lose this job, what do I eat!? I can only say I'm sorry." "But why didn't you tell me earlier? Are you telling the truth?" Li-An didn't know what to believe. "Yes, it's the truth!" White raised his voice this time. "What are you doing with me and your girlfriend at the same time?" Li-An let her anger and frustration burst through. "Let me tell you this," he cut her off. "Li-An, you are exactly my type. But the problem is we've not spent time together. I have friends who fell deeply in love at first but broke up in the end because they're not suitable." "So you mean to say your girlfriend suits you, no?" she shot back. "The difference between you and her is I've spent time with her," he said. "And so you two get along, no?" A short pause. "For now, yes," admitted White. "And what do you mean by I'm your type?" probed Li-An. "I like your hair, the way you dress, your voice, your smile, your qizhi." answered White. "But how about me as a person!?" Li-An wasn't sure what to make of his last reply. "Your qizhi means your personality as a whole, doesn't it!" White sounded impatient. "All I can say is, until we meet, let's keep in touch on LetsChat. I hope we can be like before. Look, I really have to go back to work. I'm sorry about what happened. Take care in Beijing." With that, they hung up on each other.

Li-An found herself walking aimlessly in the Sanlitun district, half-looking for the energy field Wu had described. Unable to meet White and retrieve his DNA sample, it was the only other reason she still had to be in Beijing. And maybe her only remaining hope, but a faint one at this point. She'd started from the Poly theater and began trudging along the main street towards Sanlitun Soho. But she had nothing to guide her. "I'll never find it," Li-An thought. "Unless it somehow finds me". That wasn't so unreasonable. She'd been guided this far by visions. But then what did it matter whether she found the spot, she asked herself. White was not in Beijing. She was still bothered by their conversation that morning.

Li-An had just passed Queen's café in Sanlitun Soho and stopped to survey the architecture when she saw light glimmering from underneath her left shoe. She stood there shocked for a few seconds, then nodded, knowingly. She moved both legs into what had become a small circle of light, emanating from the sidewalk. The minute she did so, scene after scene flashed in front of her eyes, as though she was watching a movie. When it ended, Li-An didn't move, but stood transfixed in the same spot for what seemed like hours, but could only have been a matter of minutes. She was finally brought back to her senses by a voice. "Are you ok?" I've been watching you. You've been standing here for a long time." She looked up into the face of a female Uniqlo employee speaking in a strong Beijing accent. "I'm sorry," replied Li-An, who quickly regained her composure and started walking fast. She kept walking until she found a narrow side street to turn into, and stopped to take out her phone. She felt compelled to text White, though not to tell him what just happened to her. What she saw. She wouldn't reveal that to anyone.

28th March 2017, 3.03 pm

"Where in Hebei are you? I'll come look for you. Since I'm already here in Beijing, I'll be a fool all the way through," wrote Li-An to White.

Grey was not coming for two days. Li-An reckoned she could take the high-speed train to Hebei, stay one (or even two) night at a hotel near where White worked, then back to Beijing.

28th March 2017, 3.07 pm

"Li-An, thank you but don't trouble yourself coming all the way here," White replied.

"There's really no place for you to sleep. Not in my dormitory, or anywhere near."

Li-An saw a cab coming towards her as she texted. She flagged it down, hopped on the cab and asked to be taken to her hotel. Li-An didn't' bother to reply to White. But back in her room, Li-An took a photo of the balcony and sent it to him.

28th March 2017, 3.54 pm

"This room comes with a balcony. You could have smoked there."

Another reason Li-An had booked that particular room was so White could smoke on the open-air balcony.

"Take care."

Li-An didn't think she was going to ever see White again, so was bidding him farewell.

"Don't just stay in the room. Go out and get some fresh air. Take good care of yourself."

White didn't get that Li-An's message was meant as a goodbye. But this misunderstanding pulled them back into communication.

29th March 2017, 6.05 pm

"Will you be working late tonight?" asked Li-An.

"Why?" replied White.

"Video chat. I brought my lingerie. The one I got in Guangzhou, and the one you like. I want to wear it, and show it to you," explained Li-An.

"I can't. Not tonight. By the time I get home it'll be almost midnight. I should be fine tomorrow. How about that?" answered White. Li-An acknowledged with *en*, the Chinese phonic sound for "yes".

The next evening

30th March 2017, 6.49 pm

"I'm ready anytime you are." Li-An had showered and put on her white sexy lingerie. She'd even dimed the lights to create a soothing ambience.

30th March 2017, 6.58 pm

"I'm still at work. We're having a meeting soon. Then dinner. I'll let you know."

"I'll wait," replied Li-An.

White finally called Li-An at about half-past ten. She'd almost fallen asleep, but with the ringing she quickly stacked two pillows on top of each other and against the bed frame. She placed her phone atop of the pillows, straightened her lingerie, and answered the call. "Ni hao." "Hi." Li-An smiled as she greeted White. "Ni hao." But White didn't give her his full attention. Instead, he was writing on a piece of paper. "Do I look good in the lingerie?" asked Li-An. "Yes, it's very sexy." White looked up, made the quick comment, and looked back down again. White's cold response changed her mood.

"I actually have something to tell you. I can't bring myself to say it. The reason why I'm here." Li-An looked sheepishly down to the corner of the screen as she spoke. "I'm.... I'm.... about to marry," Li-An saw from the corner of her eyes that White was now looking intently at the screen. "So what's going to happen to us?" White said, giving her a look of concern. "I can be with you for a short period until I marry. Is that alright with you?" An awkward pause. "Unless you don't want me anymore," Li-An added. "No, it's not that," responded White. "But don't worry. I'm not here to ruin anything." Li-An meant with White's girlfriend. "I'll be with you for the time being. But when the time comes, I'll leave. He'll be good to me despite his temper. And despite that I'm taller than him, and that he's turned grey. I'm fine with it."

"Stop it!" White shouted, which startled Li-An. "Why do you want to marry someone so much older than you!? And who's greying! And for goodness sake, you're taller than him! Why!? What does he have? Money?! "Mei you." "No." Li-An replied meekly. "Li-An, look at me." Li-An shifted her eyes back to the phone. "You're so eager to marry, huh?!" Furious, and now at a loss for words, White crossed his arms and turned his back on her. Li-An sat quietly still on the bed. A few seconds later, she called out his name. "Bai Xiang." White turned briefly to look at her, then turned back. "It's late. I still have things to do. Good night." White disengaged their video chat session as Li-An looked on.

30th March 2017, 11.28 pm

"Ai . . . I wish for you to be well. Take good care of yourself." White began his text with a sign.
"Don't reply. I want some peace."
Li-An soon fell asleep.

About an hour later

31st March 2017 12.26am

She was woken by a blip sound. She picked the phone next to her and saw that White had sent her a 7-second recording. Li-An played it. "I spent the night writing this script." As he spoke, White aimed the camera at the script lying on his bed, though she couldn't make out what it said. "I'm going to bed now." White dragged his words throughout the recording. Obviously, he was tired. Still, Li-An found White's coarse, husky voice very attractive.

"Again, I wish for you to be well. I wish you well, I wish you happiness."

"Goodnight." White ended with three "Z"s, their size increasing as each letter ascended diagonally from left to right.

Grey arrived in Beijing the next afternoon. He took the airport shuttle to Sanyuanqiao Subway Station, and walked the short distance to the Cendre Hotel. Li-An was sitting at the lobby when Grey arrived, sipping her free Earl Grey tea, an entitlement for guests who'd booked a studio apartment. They briefly greeted each other. Grey then went to the front desk and handed over his ID card to the clerk. When he was done registering, Li-An brought him to her room. Grey was impressed. This is very nice! Simple but tasteful. You have very good taste," he commented.

31ˢᵗ March 2017, 6.54 pm

"Wo xiang ni ne." I miss you." wrote Li-An to White. "Ne": A particle to reinforce the sentence preceding it. But no reply.

It was the evening of 1ˢᵗ April 2017. While Grey was watching TV, Li-An went and sat in the dressing room. She swiped her cellphone, clicked on the LetsChat App, searched for the message board that she and White shared, and started typing.

1ˢᵗ April 2017, 6.54 pm

"Ge, I heard you. The things you said the other night," wrote Li-An.
    "Just read."
    "Don't reply to me straight away."

1ˢᵗ April 2017, 6.56 pm

"You want me to be well, happy. I feel happy whenever we chat, tease each other. But I'm not perfect. And I can't destroy your life." Li-An knew very well White wouldn't understand the context to the message, especially the last two sentences, but wrote them anyway.
    "But I've fallen in love with you."

1ˢᵗ April 2017, 6.58 pm

"If you feel the same for me, I have the following suggestion."

151

1ˢᵗ April 2017, 7 pm

"Let's fall in love, shall we? Let's go all out to miss each other, find time to see each other. I'll not marry right away. We'll be together like this for as long as we can. A year, A year and half, two years . . . I will live in Kramen Island, but I'll come find you in Beijing or Hebei. But you must be honest with me. Once you find the girl you like and plan to marry, let me know. I'll go. Likewise, I'll leave you when it's time for me to go. But for now, I can't bring myself to end this."

"During this period, I'll not be with any man." Li-An had made up her mind to leave Grey if White answered "yes" to her proposition.

"Think about it."

"You only have to answer "yes" or "no". I'll give you a few days to think. If I don't hear from you, I'll take it that you're not interested. And I'll not bother you again."

The next morning, Li-An was woken up by a blip sound on her phone. White had messaged her. She picked up the phone to read the message, her back facing Grey, who was still asleep.

2ⁿᵈ April 2017, 7.42 am

"Li-An, it was almost midnight when I returned to the hostel last night. So I didn't reply you. I'm sorry. But I saw what you wrote. And I understand what you mean. In short, I want you to take good care of yourself. I don't want you to suffer in any way. Life is short. Live well in this life. My wish is that this year, next year, the year after next, every year, the rest of our lives, we will think about each other. Till the end of time."

"Because I can feel that you are a kindhearted girl. I trust my feelings about you." White added two hugs.

"It's time I get out of bed and prepare for work." (a smiley with tongue sticking out)

Her back turned to Grey, Li-An quietly let the tears stream down her face.

15 THE BITE OF REALITY

4th April 2017, 12.06 am

"The flight was delayed so I only just touched down. I'm now heading home in a cab." Li-An thought of White the moment the plane arrived at Kramen Island.

She also briefly informed Grey, who replied almost immediately. "Xin ku le." "It's been tough." White, on the other hand, did not reply.

The next day, however, White sent Li-An a photo. It showed a human hand writing on what looked like an official document. Li-An noticed at the corner a red stamp pad.

5th April 2017, 11.13 am

"My client is about to sign the contract," wrote White. "Congratulations," replied Li-An.

5th April 2017, 9 pm

Missing White, Li-An dropped him a text message that evening. "Can we video chat once or twice every month?"

5th April 2017, 9.41 pm

"Sure," White replied forty minutes later.

"But first you must promise me to take good care of yourself," continued White.

5th April 2017, 9.55 pm

"Bu yao." "I don't want!" protested Li-An playfully.

"I want to live crazily and totally carefree! This world needs fools like us. Goodnight!" Li-An knew she wasn't free in real life. But in LetsChat, she could be what she wanted. Free. Romantic. And truly young.

5th April 2017, 10.04 pm

"Xiao yang!" teased White.

"Yi ci ye hao." "Even once is good," Li-An wrote.

5th April 2017, 11.33 pm

"I will miss you, Li-An. I love you."

6th April 2017, 7.24 am

"My dear, good morning!" posted White.

"I'm off to work."

"Li-An, Ge will miss you." White added two hugs.

"I love you."

Li-An woke up to the sound of her phone. Seeing the messages were White's, she quickly scanned through and replied "Ge, I love you too."

6th April 2017, 8.09 pm

"I'm in the shower," wrote Li-An to White that same night.

"I want to be hot in love with you."

"You said "I love you" twice this morning to me. I have an urge to come to Beijing right now and make love to you."

Still in the shower, Li-An took a selfie of her face and sent it to White. She wanted to give him a wet look.

6th April 2017, 11.10 pm

"Good night. I love you," Li-An wrote to White hoping that he would reply. But he didn't.

7th April 2017, 7.20 am

"Good morning!" wrote Li-An to White the next morning.
"I think about you the moment I open my eyes," continued Li-An.

7th April 2017, 9.04 am

"Good morning, Li-An. I knocked off very late last night, so didn't reply you. The morning meeting just ended. We're getting busy."

7th April 2017, 9.05 am

Li-An posted a selfie in bed. She'd gone back to sleep after her last text but woke up as soon as she heard the familiar 'click' sound, knowing White had responded. Li-An looked a little groggy in the photo.
"I just woke up." (a smiley with rosy cheeks)

7th April 2017, 9.52 am

"I know you're hard at work." Li-An added a heart-shaped icon at the end of her text.
"Guai." "Good girl," replied White, who followed with two hugs in his next text.

For days, Li-An didn't look for White. She'd made it a point to not disturb him for a while.

3 days later

10th April 2017, 7.15 am

"Qing ai de zao shang hao." "Good morning, my love," wrote White.

"I love you," wrote Li-An, excited that White took the rare initiative to write to her first.

"Boy, you are early," replied White.

"Why don't you go back to sleep?"

10th April 2017, 7.19 am

"And I miss you," Li-An finished her sentence even as a new overlapping message from White came in.

"I'm out of bed," continued White.

"Off to work? Not resting?" By now, Li-An had gotten a sense of how taxing his work schedule was.

"It's impossible to rest now that we're getting so busy."

"Can you take a selfie and show me?" requested Li-An.

"I want to see how you look now."

10th April 2017, 8.03 am

"I'm on my way to work." (a smiley with hand over mouth).

"Li-An, sleep more. Be a good girl."

11th April 2017, 7.23 am

"Good morning, Li-An."

"This world is too small. I'll accompany you to the end of the world and every corner of the sea." "Tian ya hai jiao," wrote White who followed his message with a song recording titled "Once is Good Enough."

"I like its lyrics," White wrote.

"I miss you," Li-An replied lovingly.

11th April 2017, 7.25 am

"I'm off to work now." (A typical smiley)

White then sent Li-An a photo of himself. He'd aimed his phone at his own image in a mirror above a dresser. Excepting that his legs were blocked by hairspray bottles lying in the foreground, Li-An saw how White looked in his uniform. This time he was wearing a white shirt underneath. And he had on his usual sunglasses.

11th April 2017, 8.08 am

"I'm getting out of bed too. Be careful on the road." Li-An was starting to feel this relationship becoming more real, as though they were actually inhabiting the same space.

"You must be well," continued Li-An.

"You too." And White added two hugs.

"Once is Good Enough" was the theme song from the movie, *The Troubles of Xia Luo*, and was also known as a "warm water song", a literal translation of the three Chinese characters that made up the phrase. Li-An found an online remark connecting it to an earlier movie based on the ancient fable *Journey to the West*. The director hadn't the money to publicize the movie when it was released, which affected initial ticket sales. His fans, called "tap water" or "water soldiers", came to the director's rescue and the movie eventually became a box office hit. The director of *The Troubles of Xia Luo* decided at the last minute to include a movie soundtrack to thank his supporters. So the song "Once is Good" also became known as a warm water song. Li-An knew the reason White had sent her the song: because its title matched the statement "yi ci ye hao" ("Even once is good") which she made soon after returning from Beijing, 5th April. Obviously, White had remembered that.

11th April 2017, 10.49 pm

"I really like being 'woken up' by you in the morning. It feels like you're just by my side. I'm so blissed out. And you know what? I was taken completely by surprised when you said you love me the morning of the 5th. It was so beautiful and pure. I'm glad for this experience," Li-An wrote.

11th April 2017, 10.56 pm

"I'm also glad that we did not get to meet in Guangzhou and Beijing."

So they'd fallen in love with each other, she reflected. But over, what? Short posted phrases and icons? Or lies. At least in Li-An's case. She felt guilty, but yet again relished the tenderness she'd been denied all her life. Her first boyfriend had used her to satisfy his sexual curiosity. But it was different with White. Even their first video chat was more a fun game of seduction than anything physical, with all those added complexities.

Li-An thought back to the scenes that had flashed before her eyes at Beijing Sanlitun, when the energy field - or whatever it was - had found her. She knew even then that they were revealing her fate. And it was a future did not include White. So this love bubble would burst sooner or later. But she would make it last as long as she could. It was such a good feeling to love someone.

12th April 2017, 8.10 am

"Ge, good morning." Li-An wrote the next morning. She even added a selfie of herself still lying in bed.

"I miss you very much."

"Will you find some time next week to video chat with me?" she requested.

12th April 2017, 8.31 am

"Sure thing."

"Li-An, I miss you too."

"I'll wait for you," chirped a still sleepy Li-An.

White simply replied with a smiley. Rosy cheeks, both irises looking to the left side, and mouth in broad U-shape.

15th April 2017, 7.59 am

White sent a selfie of himself. It was a close-up, but Li-An could tell the photo was taken in a car. He was sitting in the passenger seat, and his male colleagues were in the back. White was wearing the same sunglasses, but this time he was dressed entirely in dark shades of blue, including his tie.

15ᵗʰ April 2017, 7.59 am

"Ge is on his way to work," White wrote the message within the same minute that he sent the photo.

15ᵗʰ April 2017, 8.05 am

"Don't tire yourself too much," wrote a concerned Li-An

.

15ᵗʰ April 2017, 10.27 pm

Li-An sent a selfie of her in the shower. Both breasts were exposed except for her nipples. Li-An had skillfully covered them with her upper arms.

"Naughty," White immediately replied.

"Ge has been called back to Hebei. I'm still in a meeting. Go to bed early, Li-An. Once I get to knock off early, Ge wants to see you. In the next two days or so."

Li-An became excited at White's invitation. She wanted so badly to see him onscreen. Li-An smiled, put the phone back on the side table next to her, popped an Xter pill, and immediately fell asleep.

16ᵗʰ April 2017, 9.46 am

"Let's video chat tonight," wrote White.

"I should knock off early today."

"I'll prepare and wait for you," replied Li-An.

It was thirty minutes past ten. Li-An's phone rang. The sound resembled that of a siren. She picked up the phone, placed it on the two pillows stacked on top of one another against the bed frame, and pressed the "answer" button. "Hi, Big Brother," greeted Li-An. "Oh, you're wearing that again." White was lying flat on his stomach and smoking a cigarette as he spoke. "Shi de." "Yes, that's right." Half embarrassed and half excited, Li-An looked down at her mattress. She had on the same blue one-piece satin-like lingerie that she wore for their first video chat. "Do you want to see?" Li-An shyly asked, eyes still looking down. "Lai ba." "Do it," replied

White. Slowly, Li-An loosened the button on her chest, then pulled one strap down, followed by the other, revealing her breasts. White took a drag on his cigarette and as he blew out the smoke, crushed the butt on the tray next to him. Silence. A half minute later, Li-An slowly pulled the straps to her shoulder and fastened the button. She smiled embarrassingly, trying all the while to avert White's gaze.

"Li-An, Big Brother has something to discuss with you," said White, in an unexpectedly serious tone.

"You don't want me anymore?" Li-An blurted out, worried. Now she looked straight into the screen and at White.

"No, it's not that," White replied in a comforting tone.

"Then what?" Her eyes started roving around.

"Why don't I text you instead? Once you're done reading, let me know and we will go on screen again. Ok?"

Li-An nodded and pressed the red button to disengage the session. She waited nervously for his text.

16th April 2017, 10.44 pm

"Li-An, I'm a competitive person. I also have the man's common flaw that I care about face. I can't bring myself to say it when I see you, so decided to write to you. Last year, I earned more than three hundred thousand renminbi. I used some for myself, gave some to my family to buy things, et cetera. I'm now left with about a hundred thousand. The property I'm selling now . . . there's a unit that caught my eye. The price, location, and appreciation prospect, there's no problem at all. I am thinking of buying it either for investment or my own use. But I'm short of three hundred thousand renminbi. This year, I'll be earning two to three times more than last year. But I will only get the money in October. I need your help. I will be able to return you the money by the end of the year."

Li-An's heart dropped.

16th April 2017, 11 pm

"Li-An, are you still there?" asked White fifteen minutes later. But Li-An didn't reply.

16th April 2017, 11.02 pm

"I know you can't reply straight away. I'll give you some time to think. I'll contact you again," wrote White.

16th April 2017, 11.30 pm

"Good night, Li-An. I hope in your eyes I'm someone whom you love and trust at the same time," White wrote about half an hour later. He even added a hug icon.
"How I wish you were sleeping next to me in my arms."

16th April 2017, 11.45 pm

"I do love you," Li-An wrote fifteen minutes later in reply to White.
"I know, Li-An. Go sleep."
The next morning

17th April 2017, 7.15 am

"Good morning, Li-An. Big Brother is up and starting the day."
"I miss you," She replied.
But Li-An was no longer sure that she did. Is that what it was all about? Was it ultimately money White was after? The love bubble had finally burst, but in such a crass and unexpected way. Now she recalled all the times he'd declined to physically meet. First in Guangzhou. And more recently in Beijing. As Li-An's thoughts began running wild, the phone made the familiar "click" sound. She checked and saw that White had sent her another uncharacteristically long message.

17th April 2017, 9.51 am

"To be honest, I spent the last few days thinking about whether to approach you for money. I've never asked for money from anyone. My lifestyle is such that I never depend on anyone. How many things I can do depends on how much I earn. I don't know why I actually opened my mouth to ask for money from you. I don't normally plan my budget. If I like something, I'll buy as long as I can afford it. I never plan. That is why I'm now caught in such an embarrassing situation. I'm doing this because my colleagues and manager are all investing in real estate this year. There is great prospect for this piece of land. And it's a short-term investment. Within three to four years, I'll be able to sell it and earn good profits. If I can invest in one now, I should be able to not work so hard the next couple years. I'm not a lazy person but this is one way to earn money. Those colleagues of mine who've worked a little longer already have two to three properties. All for investment. They now have a net worth upwards of five hundred thousand renminbi. They all borrowed money. From their relatives or friends. Now their property values have increased manifold. Since I've opened my mouth to ask for money from you, I hope you can help me this time. I will return you the money between November and December this year, that is in half a year's time. I hope you will not reject me, honestly."

17th April 2017, 9.57 am

"I'm going through a most difficult time now. Whoever helps me, I'll remember her for the rest of my life. You will be like delivering coal in the midst of snow. You should understand this saying. In return I will be forever grateful."

Li-An broke down in tears.

17th April 2017, 10.01 am

"What will you give me in return?" Li-An decided to challenge him.

17th April 2017, 10.08 am

"My details below:
My name is: Bai Xiang
Phone no.: 13720025962 (I've used this number for many years and will not change it. Phone numbers starting with 137 belong to the earliest batch, so I'll not change it)
I.D. number: 610621188709060431

Passport number: E85618236
This is all that I can give you."

17th April 2017, 10.10 am

"With all these you will be able to find me. Is the information enough for you?" White wrote again.

Li-An didn't answer White. She was distracted by another message. This one from Grey.

"Li-An, I want to see you. I want to know how you're doing," wrote Grey.

Grey had texted Li-An the night before, around 10 pm. He'd wanted to talk to her. Li-An, who had been waiting for White, decided to give him an excuse. "I'm tired. I'm going to bed soon. Goodnight." Now she was even less willing. She ignored his text and returned to White's message board.

17th April 2017, 10.17 am

"I can't make a decision now. I need more information."

Li-An had made up her mind not to lend him the money, but wasn't prepared to reject him.

Within seconds, White sent a picture of his passport. Li-An noticed an immaculately polished finger nail in the foreground. He'd had a female colleague hold the passport while he took the picture. She suspected White had gone to work that morning determined to buy that property. Why else would he bring a passport with him? Li-An enlarged the picture, and zoomed into White's birthdate. 7th September 1987. White was indeed ten years her junior.

"I don't know what else I can offer," White wrote.

"I need the money today, or noon tomorrow latest. The sales have started. I have to pay my company tomorrow or the day after." He was trying to push her into a quick decision, like the experienced salesman he was.

"Do you know how I'm feeling at this moment?" Li-An decided to be frank with him.

"I don't know why we have to go through this. What I'm asking is a small sum of money." Li-An was shocked by that reply. Three hundred thousand renminbi a small sum?

"I'm thinking that you don't love me, and never did" Li-An wrote back.

"Yes, I can understand. But I already told you. You're helping me. And I know you will help me. The reason being that you love me. And I know that. And I will forever remember you for this."

Li-An's heart broke more with every text.

"To be honest, I don't want to lose this opportunity. This property is a good money-making machine. Otherwise, I wouldn't be like this," White kept on.

Li-An wasn't going to send anything, but, controlling herself, decided to test him.

"Then can you tell your company to wire the money directly to my account in November, and send me their reply as proof? I need that kind of guarantee."

Just as she finished typing out those words, Li-An's phone started to ring with its familiar siren-esque tone. It was Grey calling to video chat. Li-An decided to answer him this time.

"Li-An, I need to talk to you. I didn't sleep at all last night." Indeed, Grey didn't look good.

"Ever since you got back from Beijing, we haven't been communicating. I don't think this is how a couple should behave. Are you hiding something from me?" He asked. But Li-An hesitated to reply.

"Answer me!" Grey raised his voice which startled Li-An.

"I don't love you," replied Li-An, and immediately broke down in tears. She then confessed to him about White, and that he was pestering her for money even as they spoke.

"I'm sorry," apologized Li-An as she saw Grey starting to tear himself.

"Did you make the recent trip to Beijing in order to see him?" probed Grey.

"No," Li-An lied, not wishing to hurt Grey further.

"You should forget about me. I'm not what you think I am. I got together with you because . . ." Li-An stopped before she spilled the beans.

"Because of what?" Grey asked sternly.

"I had to survive. I needed your help with my dissertation."

Li-An wouldn't have been able to find the documents or open doors on her own, she admitted. She'd gone to Chengdu and Beijing before starting her PhD program, even before she'd met Grey, and knocked on the doors of Chinese professors. They'd just turned her away. She'd begun to understand the importance of guanxi in China. Connections, or putting oneself into the right network. That's the excuse she gave Grey for their engagement.

"You say you don't love me, but we've made love so many times," Grey said, almost desperately.

"It wasn't out of love," Li-An blurted out, then looked away.

Grey, looking hurt, abruptly ended the video chat.

When she returned to the shared message board with White, Li-An saw to her horror that he'd sent her a long unbroken succession of short text messages. Before this, White had never written so much, and especially during working hours. "Shang ban." "At work," was his perennial excuse, so that Li-An wouldn't disturb or write to him in the day. But obviously, White didn't think his long texting this morning would affect his work situation. Not when three hundred thousand renminbi was involved.

"No, this will be between you and me," White responded to Li-An's last message, rejecting her call for a guarantee from his company.

"You think a transnational company like Huamanyuan will do such a thing???" Li-An noted the three question marks.

"Isn't the trust between us enough??? We know each other, no???"

"No, we don't. You don't really know who I am," Li-An instinctively shook her head as she messaged.

"Li-An, I'm not asking for millions. It's only three hundred thousand renminbi. That is sixty thousand Kramen dollars. We've known each other for so long. Why are you thinking that I'm cheating you of your money?"

"Only four months. We've known each other for four months, and through engaging in stupid online chat," thought Li-An as she read White's text.

"I repeat again. I'm borrowing from you, and you're helping me. I'll return you the money between November and December this year. I'm not asking that you give me the money. Got it?"

Before Li-An could finish reading the rest of his messages, White sent yet another one.

17th April 2017, 12.10 pm

"You have until tomorrow noon to send me the money," he demanded.

17th April 2017, 12.11 pm

"I felt very romantic last night, thinking you truly missed me. But it was for another reason you asked to video chat. Money!!!! I can't come round to this. You don't love me at all!" Li-An was tempted to delete White from LetsChat altogether.

"I love you, Li-An. Don't doubt my sincerity."

"Then can't you imagine how this makes me feel?" responded Li-An.

"I tell you what," she continued.

"You have 24 hours to come up with a plan of how I can safely lend you the money, with clear guarantees. Otherwise, I can't help you." Li-An then switched off her phone.

For the rest of the day, Li-An sat in a corner, shuddering in some combination of regret and fear. White had been an illusion. But how was she going to accomplish her mission now that Grey had left? It could spell the end of her. All of the other subjects had accomplished their missions. Everyone except Li-An was married, and had at least tried to reproduce. She was suddenly more focused on the repercussions of failure. "They'll turn you off" Evans had said. What exactly would they do? Stop the Xter pills, so she'd end up looking like him? Or worse? Li-An remembered the professor warning her against falling in love. For hours, Li-An stared blankly into space feeling that all hope was lost. It was only when dusk fell that she switched her phone back on. The message board she shared with White was inundated with more of his text messages.

17th April 2017, 12.35 pm

"All I can give you are my identity details. I don't know what else to give."

17th April 2017, 12.45 pm

"I've never borrowed money before, so I don't know what else I need to do. You tell me."

17th April 2017. 12.55 pm

"Li-An, the question is whether or not you want to lend the money. And if you trust me enough to do so. I've given you all my personal details. There's no way I can run away. There's no way I'll commit a crime for this little amount of money." (An emoticon with eyes closed and a drop of sweat on one side of the face)

"Am I so untrustworthy?" (Wide-eyed emoticon with a question mark above head)

17th April 2017, 1.05 pm

"With all the information I've given you, can't you at least feel my sincerity? I'm for real. We even had a meal together. Isn't that enough proof? How can you not feel safe? What will make you feel safe?"

Li-An couldn't help but laugh at White's last text. They had one meal, and he expected her to give him sixty thousand Kramen dollars? Li-An also noticed that White had used the word "feel", not "see". Suddenly, she was struck by the reality that she had loved this man based on her own self-generated feelings, nothing else.

17th April 2017, 1.20 pm

"Li-An, I love you."

17th April 2017, 1.24 pm

"Li-An, are you still there?"

17th April 2017, 1.35 pm

"I didn't drink a single drop of water today."
"I'm calling my clients even as I'm writing to you."
"I'm making a lot of sales this time. I can say for sure I will be the top salesman for this financial year." (An arm bent at the elbow showing prominent muscles and hand in fist)

17th April 2017, 2.48 pm

"You are not helping me, are you?"
Li-An didn't reply, and White didn't pursue it further.

17th April 2017, 6.10 pm

White finally broke the long silence between them.
"What do you want, Li-An. Just tell me. I feel very uncomfortable now. If you can help me this time, I will make the purchase. Otherwise, I'll just drop the idea."

17th April 2017, 6.21 pm

"Ever since I said "I love you", I've decided to be with you for the rest of my life. You have a place in my heart, remember that. Don't let this affect our relationship. If you decide to help me, I'll owe you one. If you decide not to help me, it's your decision. We don't owe each other anything anyway."
She stopped reading and headed for the bathroom. Li-An realized she desperately needed to shower and freshen up. Never mind that she hadn't eaten anything that day. Li-An had lost all appetite. Half an hour later, she emerged from the bathroom, put on her pajamas, blew her hair dry, and picked up the phone. She decided to have one last conversation with White before going to bed.

17th April 2017, 7.25 pm

"I love you, though I'm saying this for the last time. I'm sorry I can't help you," wrote Li-An.

"You just need to give me half a year's time. I'll surely return you the money." It was futile. His whole mind was on the property.

"Is that house so important to you?" asked Li-An.

"It's not that the house is important, Li-An. It's the opportunity to invest," White wrote back.

"This is a very good investment. The location is suitable. I've thought everything through. This will be a short-term investment."

"I've been working so damn hard last year. With this, I can rest easy for the next two to three years. How important do you think this investment is to me?" White asked rhetorically.

"I wouldn't know," answered Li-An. She was recalling how she'd suffered and worked hard all her life, something he'd done only a single year.

"You know, Li-An."

"But why so urgent?" she probed.

"Because we have to make the payment within two days." White answered.

"Aren't my identification details enough? And by the way, I don't expect you to do anything bad with them."

"Ha!" Li An exclaimed out loud. Now he was doubting her honesty?

"I hope you will give me an answer by 6pm tomorrow evening."

"Oh, so now the deadline is no longer noon tomorrow," Li-An thought, as she jerked her head back in surprise. It was now clear that White was taking her for a qing chi. A love fool.

"I loved you so much . . ." Li-An wrote in despair. If not for the fact that she was totally exhausted, she would have cried her heart out.

Li-An switched off her phone, hid it under the pillow next to the one that she normally used, and took a pill. Within seconds she was knocked out.

The next morning, Li-An woke up and stared blankly into the ceiling for a long time. She then turned to look at the side table on her right. There was no phone. Li-An suddenly recalled that she'd placed it under the pillow next to her, found it, and switched it back on. White had finally stopped texting her. Instead, she found a message from Grey. "Li-An, I love you," Grey wrote. "I want to be your support. Let me know how I can help."

16 THE FINAL EXIT

For the next two months Li-An mostly stayed off LetsChat, but would occasionally post pictures of herself, and then log out. When she'd log in again, she'd see that White had viewed her posting and indicated 'like' by clicking the heart-shaped icon. He did that for every single one of her photos.

One night, missing White, Li-An took out her Apple laptop, opened it, clicked on Microsoft Word and started writing.

Ge, it's the 29th of June, Wednesday, 8.25pm. Two months have passed. Tonight, I feel like writing you.

It's been a long time since I called you Ge. It sounds nice, doesn't it? Makes me feel close to you.

Ge, I miss you very much. But I'm also hurt and confused. I've been trying very hard to let go of you, but I can't. I've also been asking myself why that's so? After all, we only met twice. Once in the plane, and once in Beijing. We've not spent time together, just like you said. So, where is the love? Is it because of what happened in our first video chat? Maybe. But that's quite unbelievable, isn't it? We didn't physically touch, but after that session, I felt bonded to you.

Ge, what am I to you? In our second video chat, before my trip to Beijing in March, you said "You don't know me and I don't know you." But when I asked if you liked me, you nodded your head. So, where does this feeling of fondness come from? You stood me up in Beijing. I called you. Your reply was "What a girl." You sounded dismissive on the phone. Why that tone? And what does "What a girl" mean?

On 6ʰ April, you said "I love you". But then you asked for 300,000 yuan. Is that why you said "I love you", so that I'd give you the money? And you were confident that I would. The reason you gave was because I love you. "You love me, so you'll give me the money," you said the day you pestered me for the cash. Is this what love is to you? It comes with a price?

I fell in love with you knowing it would not last. All I wanted was to know how it feels to be in love. Pure, unadulterated love that can only happen in a world divorced from reality. A vacuum which I found in LetsChat. Despite the surreality, I finally know what it feels like to be in love. To miss someone, to get all excited when the person responds to you, your messages, to know there is someone in this world that cares for you, to hear (or "read" in our case) "I love you" from the other party, and not to mention the sadness from failing to see the person you love in the flesh. It was a combination of sweetness, bittersweet, bliss, and sorrow. I had a taste of all these emotions in just four months. Until you burst it.

All this while, I knew well that my love for you bordered on fantasy. Your request for money drew me back to reality. Yet I still harbor feelings of love for you. I don't think you will understand this, but I'm running out of time. Soon I have to go. Either by deleting you from my account or deleting myself from the world of LetsChat. But before that, Ge, I'd like to see you. Only by meeting can I know whether everything that's been said, been done on LetsChat has any reality at all.

Li-An

Li-An didn't send the letter right away but slept on it. The next day, after much deliberation, she decided to send it off that very night. When she was done, Li-An immediately logged off LetsChat and told herself she wouldn't hang on the possibility of his reply. But impelled by curiosity, she logged back into LetsChat two days later. There were six message alerts, all from White. She clicked onto their message board and saw that White had written her the very same night she'd posted the letter.

30th June 2017, 10.45 pm

"Are you still here?" asked White.

Li-An checked the time. The message was written fifteen minutes after her own posting. Clearly, White had read the letter before replying.

30th June 2017, 10.54 pm

"We are exceptionally busy now. There was an official launch five days ago. There were 800 units on sale. There are 36 of us in the team. I sold the most. 62 units. And over a period of 9 months. Not bad huh? 9 months of hard work. I'll earn a total of 370,000 *yuan* in commission for this. I didn't buy that property after all. Since you left, I've been blaming myself. I kept asking myself why I asked you for money. For a long time, I couldn't figure that out. And the only reason I can offer is I really wanted that property. I was wrong. Please forgive me for causing you hurt. The only thing I can do is say "I'm sorry".

30th June 2017, 11.15 pm

"I believe you know how long it's been since our first video chat. You asked if I wanted to see you, and you took off your clothes. You instructed me not to take pictures of you. But I did. I had no evil intentions. I only wanted to keep them for memory's sake, to remember our first video chat moments. And to look at them when I miss you. What you see here are images I took of you."

White followed the message with three naked pictures of Li-An, all taken the night they video-chatted for the first time.

"I want you to see them because I want you to know what kind of person I am. I want you to know that I've not and will never do anything bad with these pictures. All I want is to look at them when I think about you."

"I don't have a perverted side. I just want to keep those beautiful moments." (a regular smiley)

"I hope you will still share with me both the sad and happy things in your life. Take good care of yourself."

Li-An did not reply.

Two months later

30ᵗʰ August 2017, 2.20 pm

"*Ge*, I know you replied to my letter two months ago. I also know you have been seeing my postings. I've been thinking. You are so capable. Go find a pretty girl, one who can give you a child. Right from the start, I shouldn't have engaged with you. After the dinner in Beijing, we should have gone our separate ways," wrote Li-An one night.

30ᵗʰ August 2017, 2.38 pm

"To be honest," White replied, "I'd carefully scrutinize every picture every time I came across your posting. Each and every one of them. There are things I want to tell you, just that I don't know where to start. But I miss you. That's all."

30ᵗʰ August 2017, 3.54 pm

"Thank you. I miss you too," wrote Li-An.

"But I'm running out of time. Try your best to forget me, will you?"

White sent a picture of him talking on his cellphone. Either he'd chosen to ignore her last text message, or he missed it.

30ᵗʰ August 2017, 4.48 pm

"A colleague of mine sent me this today. It was taken early this year." (a smiley looking puzzled)

Li-An didn't reply White. Sensing her unusual reticence, he wrote the next morning.

1ˢᵗ September 2017, 9.34 am

"Li-An, take good care of yourself. Once I have the chance, I will go to Kramen Island and look for you. Of course, when you have the opportunity to come to Beijing let me know. I want to see you too. Take care."

1st September 2017, 9.51 am

"I can't wait too long. My situation is different from normal people," Li-An wrote back.

1st September 2017, 9.52 am

"I'll find you as soon as I have the chance," White wrote reassuringly.
"I want to know if you love me," She replied.
"I love you and I want to see you so badly. But I just don't understand why we could never meet. It's not that I don't want to see you. Maybe it's our fate. But I have this feeling that if we have each other in our hearts, one day we'll certainly meet," explained White.

1st September 2017, 10.01 am

"I don't know what life in the future will be. I only know that I love you," Li-An wrote back.
"Li-An, I know. Take good care of yourself," responded White.
"Remember, I can't wait too long."

Li-An contacted Evans on her RexPad and told him about her trip to China, the meeting with Wu, and finding the energy field at Sanlitun Soho. She even revealed to him the seven scenes she saw when she'd stepped inside.
"You told me Professor Wu could help me, but all he did was send me to a place where I experienced more visions that I don't understand. Are they my fate, those scenes? There was no White. I had no one to love. I was all alone," Li-An cried out desperately.
"You won't be alone if you complete your mission now. It's still not too late," answered Evans. He kept quiet about her visions.

"But remember, your 40th birthday is coming up soon. December," he reminded her.

"Is that all you can say? I don't want either the fate in the vision or the one you've chosen for me. I want my own life!" Li-An shouted vehemently.

"What I'm offering you is the best that can ......"

"What you're offering me is hell!" she interrupted. By now, she was crying uncontrollably.

"Oh, Li-An," Evans' voice was suddenly sympathetic rather than commanding, but she'd have none of it.

"If you and Professor Wu can't save me, I'll do it myself!" Li-An cut off the transmission.

Looking resigned, Evans let out a sigh and picked up the phone receiver.

"Yes, Professor," answered Samantha on the other end.

"I just heard from Li-An," he said. It's not good. Prepare Plan B," instructed Evans.

A month and half later

18th October 2017, 2.44 pm

"Li-An, how's life? Have you been busy? Are you happily spending your time every day? Next week, I'm going to Hebei Langfang city. I'll be there for a week. 23rd October that is Monday all the way till 29th October. Although it's a work trip, but there's actually nothing much to do. I probably only need to clock 2 to 3 hours of work each day, but after that I'm free. I wonder if you can take time off that week to see me?" White wrote.

18th October 2017, 4.14 pm

"Give me some time to think about it. It's a little sudden." Li-An wavered about replying to White at first, but in the end responded.

White replied with an ok hand sign.

18th October 2017, 4.59 pm

"*Ge*, I have three questions: 1. Are we meeting in Langfang city? Or are we transferring to another place? I'm asking you this because I need to take into account flight timings. 2. Is it better that I fly to Beijing first? Or is it more convenient to get to Langfang from Beijing than Tianjin? 3. And are you certain this time? I don't want to be disappointed again," Li-An asked.

18th October 2017, 5.09 pm

"It takes only 21 minutes to get to Langfang station from Beijing via the high-speed train. Once you reach the station, I'll be there waiting for you. We'll then take a bus from there to Langfang University Town. It'll take around an hour or so," replied White.

"All you need to do once you reach Beijing is take the high-speed train to Langfang station," he wrote again.

18th October 2017, 5.15 pm

"What time do you arrive in Langfang on the 23rd?" asked Li-An.
"Let me think," White replied.
"I should arrive in the morning or noon."
"If you can come, we will go to University Town together."
"How about accommodation?" Li-An needed more information.
"My company's dormitory. It's only me and nobody else. But I've never been there. If the dormitory is not to your liking, we'll go check into a hotel."

Li-An again remembered that she was older than White and that he would under no circumstances see her passport.

18th October 2017, 5.24 pm

"I can't confirm right now. Most likely, I can only come on the 24th. If that's the case, I'll book a hotel and you find me there."

18th October 2017, 6.44 pm

"If you are sure about going, I will go buy the air-tickets. Find me in the hotel either on the 23rd or 24th, ok? Nothing should go wrong

176

this time. I miss you. I have a lot of things to say to you," wrote Li-An.

"I am certain this time." White replied confidently.

For the rest of the day, Li-An researched about Langfang city. She'd never been there and her curiosity was peaked. She scoured through sleepeasy.com for a decent hotel. She saw one with a very high rating. Golden Elephant Golf Hotel. Li-An looked through the pictures of the different room types, and was particularly drawn to the deluxe suite, especially the white marble tiles and flooring in the bathroom. She went ahead to book the room, given that it came with free cancellation. But Li-An couldn't bring herself to confirm and purchase the air tickets. She told White she didn't want to be disappointed again, but the truth was more complicated. She missed White no doubt, but mostly as a respondent in LetsChat. Increasingly, she felt his physicality was no longer necessary. And if so, what then was she in love with? A person or an unfulfilled desire? Or maybe her meeting with Evans made Li-An realize it was time to come to terms with reality. Yet ever since Li-An gave herself up to become Evans' 'human subject', nothing seemed very real.

18th October 2017, 9.55 pm

"Li-An, I hope you haven't bought the air-tickets," White wrote to Li-An many hours later.

"No, I haven't," answered Li-An.

"Are you cancelling again?" She asked.

"You can be honest with me."

Fifteen minutes later, White sent Li-An a screenshot of correspondences between him and what looked like an employee from his company's headquarters. White had scratched out the headshot to protect the other party's privacy. Before Li-An could read the contents, White sent a follow-up message.

18th October 2017, 10.12 pm

"I was told tonight not to go to Langfang but instead help out at Nan Da Gang. Nan Da Gang is in Beijing and we have a showroom there. It's likely that I'll be busy there. Unlike Langfang." explained White.

"I was very happy when the order was made for me to go to Langfang this morning. I thought we could finally spend time together. But now..."

"We can wait for the next opportunity. I'm sorry, Li-An."

18th October 2017, 10.21 pm

"You should feel how much I want to see you. In our line of work, we are extremely busy. There's basically no time to rest. I'll inform you when the next opportunity comes."

Li-An was relieved deep down, but nevertheless expressed regret in her next response.

18th October 2017, 10.36 pm

"Today I was listening to the song "I want you". It contains the lyrics 'The night is too tense, the hours too long. My love, I'm in a faraway land, looking up at the moon.' As I listened, I began to tear," she wrote.

18th October 2017, 10.44 pm

White replied with two hug icons.

"Luckily you didn't buy the air-tickets. Otherwise, I wouldn't know what to do."

"It's been almost a year now," wrote Li-An who was referring to the time since they first met.

18th October 2017, 10.47 pm

"Yes. Time flies, doesn't it," replied White.

Li-An wrote out the entire song lyrics on their shared message board.

A month later

18th November 2017, 8.35 am

"Maybe we simply can't let go of each other. Maybe we have to meet. Even once." Li-An was reminded of the song "Once is Good Enough" that White sent her months back.

"I have a suggestion. Big brother, shall we meet this month? I'm really running out of time."

18ᵗʰ November 2017, 9.47 am

White replied with three emoticons all looking puzzled.
"What?" asked Li-An.

18ᵗʰ November 2017, 9.49 am

"I simply have no time to meet you. Think for a second. My average sleep hours are about 6 these days. The rest of the time are spent working and commuting. There's no way I can meet you. I can't even take leave," wrote White.

"But December will be too late," replied Li-An.

"The nature of my job is such that I have no say in the planning of my schedule. There will be another launch at the end of the month, and when it ends, I have to settle all kinds of things. Where my company will post me for my next assignment, I've no idea. Do you understand?"

Li-An's heart sank. She knew now that they'd never meet again.

18ᵗʰ November 2017, 9.57 am

"There's exposed scalp the size of a finger nail at the back of my head." (a troubled looking emoticon. Eyes drooping and hands resting on both cheeks)

"You go and do what you need to do. When I'm not busy I'll inform you. And if you still want to come to China or if I have the time, I'll find you. Then we'll meet, alright?" He continued to write. Li-An thought White sounded too casual, even dismissive.

"It's no use if you come now. I knock off every night at about 11pm, and wake up every morning at about 6am. I can't spend much time with you. In the day, you have nothing to do. I can't be selfish. So I think you should wait till I'm free."

18th November 2017, 10.10 am

"..." wrote White. He must be wondering why Li-An didn't respond.

18th November 2017, 10.47 am

"Even if we meet next spring holiday, you'll always be busy, year after year. Does it make any sense, what we're doing? Can you have a sustainable relationship via online chat? And don't you have actual opportunities around you? I never dared ask that, but there it is. I know you're busy and tired. I've held out for long enough. I need to go. Please do not 'like' my postings from now on," Li-An finally replied.

18th November 2017, 11 am

"How I wish we could go back to early this year. I was so freely in love then. Now, it seems like everything has changed."

18th November 2017, 11.10 am

"I will delete you from my account at the end of the year. Please forgive me but I have to go. You said you have things to tell me but do not know where to start. You still have a chance to do so."

Later in the evening, Li-An sat down and wrote White her thoughts in a Microsoft Word document. Her real thoughts. Thoughts she'd have as a normal woman unbridled by the burden of her age and secret.

18th November 2017, 7.03 pm

"Read it when you get back." instructed Li-An on their LetsChat board.

You asked in the Beijing restaurant what type of man I liked. Then, my answer was "I don't know."

I'll answer you now. I want a man who loves and protects me, and has a good character. Of course, I'll have to love him too.

180

I made you into that person. But you've hurt me so deeply.

This morning, you said "I can't be selfish." But right from the start, you have been. You pursued me even though you have a girlfriend, and made me fall in love with you. You know your work is all-consuming, yet you continually promised to carve out time for me. In March when I went to find you in Beijing, you were still in Hebei. You didn't even inform me. You made me wait an entire day, and I had to call you to ask for an explanation. And if you're not selfish, you would not have asked for money in April. Can't you understand what a blow that dealt me?

I no longer harbor hopes of us getting together. I don't want to be so hard on myself anymore. Let me go.

Except for the first video chat, our relationship so far has been nothing but chat. I don't want to write anymore.

Also, you want me to wait till you're free to meet. In between, we don't communicate. How natural is this? When we do meet eventually, what do you think will be the scenario? We'll be strangers, not lovers, don't you think?

I want a passionate, messy relationship. I want to be playful, like I was earlier this year. But now I feel so distant from you. Like a wild horse that's been tamed and corralled. I'm even afraid to find you. I'm not sure anymore I even want to see you.

I told you I can only be in this relationship for a short period. This year is indeed coming to an end. I've been revolving around you, missing you for close to a year. It's time I stop.

You said you have things to tell me. You can still do so between now and 31ˢᵗ December. But I'm no longer going to wait for that.

Losing your hair is no small matter. You need to maintain your handsome self. Rest well when you have the chance.

It was the morning of 5th December 2017. Li-An was at Grey's house in Hangzhou. Grey had gone to work. Li-An took out the two new sim cards that she'd told him to get for her before coming to Hangzhou. She earlier lied that she'd lost her old sim card. There was a promotion at the neighborhood telco company and Grey got a free card on top of the one he bought. Li-An inserted one of the two sim cards into her Samsung Galaxy S6. She clicked onto Messages, keyed in White's phone number which she'd noted down before deleting him from LetsChat, typed a string of words, and sent off the SMS.

5th December 2017, 11.59 am

"The tone of my last letter was harsh. I'm sorry. I deleted you from LetsChat earlier than I said I would. I'm sorry about that too."

Li-An then pressed the 'send' icon. She made sure to check that the SMS was sent successfully before removing the sim card from her phone. Li-An made a small mark on the card to indicate to herself that it was already used.

Three days passed. Li-An was sitting in the living room of her hotel room in Hangzhou. She'd earlier complained about feeling cold in Grey's house, so he checked her into West Lake Sanshe Boutique Inn. There was no central heating in Hangzhou and the electric fireplace Grey had ordered through Taobao was not arriving until a few days later. The décor in the boutique hotel resembled the wooden furnishings of the Cendre Hotel in Beijing. The room, named "leftover snow" (Can Xue), was a huge 55 square meter family suite. Li-An particularly loved the window seat in the entrance hall. When alone, she'd sit there either reading or fiddling with the second, unused sim card and contemplating whether to send White another text, and if so, what she'd say. Days passed but Li-An couldn't think of anything to tell him.

It was the night of 24th December 2017. Christmas Eve. "I still don't like that insincere kiss." Grey lightly tapped Li-An's nose. He pulled the condom off his now flaccid penis, tied a knot around it and threw it onto the floor next to his side of the bed. They'd moved back to Grey's apartment. "I'm a *da jiaoshou* (high status professor) and you are just a small-time researcher. But when you're here, I have to keep you company," said Grey as he lay back in bed, letting her know that she was taking him away from his work. But his words no longer had any effect on Li-An.

25th December 2017. 6pm. Li-An decided to write White using her last sim card.

25ᵗʰ December 2017, 6.54 pm

"I'm returning to Kramen Island tomorrow. I want to tell you one more thing before I do. *I am not what you think I am.* Whether you truly love me or not, I also want you to know that my feelings for you were genuine and real. It's exactly a year since we first met. On this Christmas night, so I'm writing to wish you all the best. I will not find you after this. The reason I deleted you from LetsChat was so that you can go and find true happiness. Goodbye."

But soon after she sent the text off, the message "You've come to the mainland?" came sliding down the top of her Samsung Galaxy S6. It was from White. Through LetsChat he'd quickly made a friend request, allowing him to communicate with her. Li-An didn't accept his friend request, nor returned his message.

30ᵗʰ December 2017. 11.30pm. In half an hour, Li-An would turn forty. Back at Kramen Island in her own apartment, she went back and forth between the three horizontally-aligned dots that formed the right icon on White's profile page and deliberating whether to press "block". She was still fiddling with the command options when, in front of her eyes, his profile just vanished.

Li-An quickly messaged Grey, ignoring his earlier birthday message to her, and coaxed him into helping her experiment with the LetsChat settings, without telling him why. First, she'd delete him. Then he'd make a friend request, followed by a message. Any message. A minute later, he'd delete her. No, that wasn't the correct formula. Ok, start over. They'd add each other back, only that this time Li-An would delete him. But Grey's profile didn't vanish as White's just had. Something else was wrong.

Had he sensed what she was feeling, and removed her before she did him? But hadn't the experiment with Grey ruled out that scenario? Was it a technical glitch? Or worse, had he reported her, and had her permanently blacklisted?

What did it really matter? She needed it to end. What did it matter who's fault it was? Slowly, she opened her laptop, went into YouTube and searched for Deborah Brown's version of "Fools Rush In".

As the song was playing, Li-An picked up the RexPad lying next to her side. With trembling hands and face soaked in tears, Li-An found and instituted the "abort" command. It would signal Evans, and whoever was behind Evans, that she was finished with their project.

A Year Later

One morning, Li-An woke up and saw three voicemail alerts on her cellphone. She got out of bed and dialed a four-digit number to access the messages. She was mainly expecting them to be sales calls, when she heard a familiar voice.

26th December 2019, 9.33 am

". . . Who's that you're calling?"

"Someone from Kramen Island . . . I find her . . . just calling her for a chat . . . I know her . . . I've saved this number but . . . don't know how to call." She recognized this as White's voice talking to a stranger.

26th December 2019, 9.35 am

"Try dialing the number again."

26th December 2019, 9.35 am

". . . shi shui?" "Who's that?" It was the same stranger's voice

"Kramen Island. I have a friend there." It was White's voice now, speaking to someone near him, as he waited for Li-An to pick up.

"Ahh-ha" the other person replied, not fully believing it was just a casual friend White was trying to contact.

13th April 2019, 9.25 am

Silence on the other end.

Li-An checked the caller details and took down the number. She then quickly logged into LetsChat, clicked on Contacts, selected "New Friends" at the top, and searched for White's headshot, which was there from the last time he contacted her. She pressed on his photo, and saw that White still had his contact number up for advertising purpose. Li-An compared the two phone numbers. They were the same.

That night, Li-An sent a text message to White through her Kramen number.

13ᵗʰ April 2019, 10.50 pm

"I loved you. Very much. Even if it was in LetsChat. But I don't wish to go back to those days. Let's move on. To be honest, you've always been in my heart. Don't find me again. Forget about me. Only remember the me in the plane and at the restaurant in Beijing. Be well. Don't reply to this. And take care."

Li-An never heard from White again. But she finally knew one thing for sure. He'd tried to find her. White did love her.

The Scenes Li-An saw at Sanlitun Soho, Beijing

Scene One: A team of scientists arrived at Li-An's apartment and took her away.

Scene Two: Li-An was back at Sentacruz in Evans' lab.

Scene Three: Li-An was lying on the surgical table and surrounded by Evans and his counterparts. There were machines, many machines and every part of Li-An's body was hooked to them.

Scene Four: Li-An was in a state of unconsciousness for a long time. Maybe a year.

Scene Five: When Li-An finally woke, Evans was by her side.

Scene Six: Evans drew pictures with his hands, as though describing a place Li-An would soon be going.

Scene Seven: Li-An was in a spherical structure, surrounded by lush greenery. Outside were only clouds.

The End